☆ American Girl®

Like Sisters

Emma Moves In

By Clare Hutton

Scholastic Inc.

For Fiona, Elise, and Lila, my daughter and nieces.

Published by Scholastic Inc., *Publishers since 1920.* SCHOLASTIC and associated logos are trademarks and/or registered trademarks of Scholastic Inc. The publisher does not have any control over and does not assume any responsibility for author or third-party websites or their content.

Book design by Maeve Norton

? americangirl.com/service

Library of Congress Cataloging-in-Publication Data available
ISBN 978-1-338-11499-7

10 9 8 7 6 5 4 3 2 1   17 18 19 20 21

Printed in the U.S.A.   23
First printing 2017

Chapter One

Things We Absolutely HAVE To Do:

1. Have a cookout

Well, that will be easy, Emma thought, wiggling her feet under the airline seat in front of her. By the time she and her parents finally got to Waverly, Uncle Luis would be flipping burgers on the grill while her mom's twin sister, Aunt Alison, and all the cousins arranged salads and desserts on the big outdoor trestle table.

Last year, her family had gotten there the evening before the annual family barbecue, and Emma and her two favorite cousins, twins Natalia and Zoe, had made up their own brownie recipe. They mixed in not just walnuts and chocolate chips, but dried pineapple, coconut, raisins, peanuts, and marshmallows. It had been Natalia's idea—Zoe had been skeptical, and Emma had thought maybe they should play it safe and follow the real recipe—but Natalia had insisted, and she'd been right. The brownies had been delicious. Emma's mouth watered at the memory.

2. Swim

Back home in Seattle, the water was too cold to swim in the ocean. Emma swam in indoor swimming pools, competing in relays and races. It was fun, and she was good at it. She liked the smell of chlorine and the stretch of her muscles. Swimming in the warm, sun-splashed water of the Chesapeake Bay with Natalia and Zoe was even better, though.

3. Sparklers

At night after the barbecue, everyone—even the grown-ups—would light sparklers out in the front yard of Zoe and Natalia's house, writing their names in light. It was tradition, and their family cared about tradition.

4. Bonfire on the beach

Some evening this week, when the weather was just right, they would build a fire of driftwood on the beach and toast marshmallows to make s'mores. Natalia liked hers so dark they were almost black, and Zoe preferred hers untoasted, but Emma would turn hers patiently until they were a perfect, even golden brown all the way around.

5. Knitting with Grandma Stephenson

Over Christmas, Grandma had started all three of them making scarves. Emma had chosen blue and white; Zoe, black and purple; and Natalia, red and turquoise. Emma had tried to finish the scarf on her own after she and her parents had gone back home, but the yarn had gotten tangled and she'd dropped too many stitches. Finally, she'd given up in frustration. It was too hard, and not as much fun by herself.

A pang went through Emma's chest at the thought of her grandmother. Back in the spring, Grandma Stephenson had fallen on the stairs of Seaview House, her big, wonderful Victorian home, and broken her hip. She was okay—everyone said she was going to be just fine—but she had left Seaview House and moved in with Zoe and Natalia's family, where their other grandma, Uncle Luis's mom, Abuelita, already lived.

Emma's mom had told her the living situation was only temporary, but it had been going on for months now. What if Grandma wasn't really okay? No, her mom wouldn't have said Grandma was going to be fine unless it was true.

But the beautiful house where generations of Emma's family had lived was shuttered and silent. Emma's mom said that Seaview House would be too big for Grandma Stephenson to take care of by herself even when she was fully recovered.

At the thought of Seaview House empty, Emma felt her throat go tight, and she swallowed back the feeling before it turned into tears. It would be silly to cry over a *house* when the important thing was that Grandma was okay. Determined not to think about Seaview House, she turned back to her list.

Emma hesitated, her pencil resting on the paper, not sure about whether to leave knitting on the list. They could knit just as well in the living room of Natalia and Zoe's house as they had in the parlor at Seaview House, of course. But maybe Grandma didn't feel like doing projects anymore since she'd been hurt. Should she scratch that one out?

Even if Grandma hadn't changed, knitting wasn't really a summer thing, and Natalia and Zoe might have already finished their scarves with Grandma while Emma wasn't there. Emma pushed away the fleeting thought, *Not fair.* She knew she couldn't expect everyone in Waverly to just wait for her to come back before doing anything fun together.

Next to her, Emma's dad gave a little snore, and she glanced up as he slouched farther down against the airplane window, his glasses perched crookedly on his nose and his mouth open. Emma's mom looked up from her laptop screen at the same time and caught Emma's eye just as her dad snorted. They both giggled.

"He's been working hard on the new menu," her mom said. "This nap is just what he needs. He'll be ready to ride the waves with you girls by the time we get there."

Emma grinned. Her dad had the most ridiculous bathing suit—bright pink with wild purple and turquoise tropical flowers on it—but she liked how he came out into the water or onto the beach in his crazy bathing suit and played with them, instead of just hanging out with the other grown-ups. Last summer, he'd helped them and Zoe and Natalia's little brothers build a huge sand castle with a pebble-covered drawbridge and turrets reaching up to the sky.

She felt a sudden surge of affection for her parents. She liked their tight little unit of three: her mother, her father, and herself.

But sometimes she couldn't help envying Zoe and Natalia for having not just their parents and each other, but also their little brothers (even if Tomás and Mateo were bratty sometimes), and Grandma Stephenson, and Abuelita, and living near Uncle Dean and Aunt Bonnie, whose own kids were mostly away at college and brand-new jobs. They had tons of family, right in their town. Right in their *house*.

They—the whole of her mom's side of the family, except for Emma and her parents—all lived in Waverly, a small town on the Chesapeake Bay, where the family had lived for generations. Natalia and Zoe went to the school where Emma's mom and their mom (Aunt Alison) had gone, along with their brother (Uncle Dean). The school was right down the street from Seaview House, where her mom's grandparents, and more generations before that, had lived.

It must be nice to *belong* somewhere so much that everyone knew you and you knew every inch of the whole town. Emma lived in Seattle now, but two years ago they'd lived in San Francisco, before her mom got a job at a different law firm. Natalia and Zoe had lived in the same house their whole lives.

Emma's mom went back to her computer screen, squinting at a long, boring-looking work document. And Emma picked up her pencil and looked down at her list again.

6. Finish the Violet story

She and Natalia had started a story last summer—all about a girl named Violet who had a talking dog that only Violet could understand and the trouble he'd gotten her into. They had laughed a lot writing it, and Zoe had drawn really funny pictures of steam coming out of Violet's ears because she was so angry and of her innocent-faced dog looking as if he had no idea what had happened or *why* everything was such a mess.

Did Natalia still have the story? They hadn't had time to work on it over Christmas. A little ball of anxiety expanded in Emma's chest. There was never enough *time*. In just a week, she'd be on a plane heading back to Seattle again.

The pilot's voice came over the intercom, interrupting her thoughts. "We're now approaching our final descent into Baltimore. Please return your seatbacks to their upright position and secure tray tables to the seatback in front of you."

There was a ton more she'd meant to write, but she was out of time again. Quickly, Emma scribbled the most important thing.

7. Cousin pact

There were so many more things she could have listed, so many things she wanted to fit into the one week they'd have with the rest of the family. But they'd make time for the pact.

She latched the tray table and put her seat upright as her mom shut down her laptop. Next to her, her dad yawned himself awake.

"How're you doing, kiddo?" he asked. "Excited to get to the house and see everybody?"

"Yeah," said Emma. She folded her list and stuffed it into the pocket of her backpack. "I just wish we could stay longer this time." She saw her parents exchange a look and added, "I know we can't. It would be fun to be with Natalia and Zoe for longer, though."

She understood why they could only come to Waverly for a few days over Christmas and for a week in the summer. Her dad was the head chef at Harvest Moon, a restaurant specializing in comfort food in Seattle, and her mom was an environmental lawyer who worked to protect the wetlands. They didn't get much time off, and Waverly was far away from Seattle. Her parents had gone over it with her a million times when she was younger and didn't understand why she couldn't see her cousins more often.

"There's a lot of stuff I want to do when we're there," she tried to explain, "and I know I won't see Natalia and

Zoe again till Christmas. I try to cram everything in, but there's never quite enough time."

Emma's dad patted her back, and her mom reached out and tucked a strand of Emma's long hair behind her ear. "We never get quite enough time with the people we love," she said sympathetically, "but try not to worry about deadlines and fitting everything you want to do in. Just concentrate on spending time with your cousins and having fun."

Emma nodded, feeling anticipation begin to spread through her. She *would* have fun. The plane's wheels hit the runway with a bump, and she realized that the whole golden, glorious week with the family was spread out before her, about to begin.

By the time their rental car pulled into the drive at Natalia and Zoe's house, Emma was vibrating with excitement. Through the window, she saw Zoe and Natalia running down the steps from the wide porch, their family's old sheepdog, Riley, ambling slowly after them. As the car came to a stop, Natalia was already pulling at the handle of the back door.

"Girls! Careful!" Emma's mom scolded, but Emma yanked her seat belt off and tumbled out into the sunshine and her cousin's tight hug.

"You're here! You're here!" Natalia shouted. Her hair was dripping wet—she'd already been swimming today, clearly—and she smelled like sunscreen and ocean water. She had pulled a T-shirt and shorts on over her wet bathing suit, and they were damp and cool.

Zoe crossed the lawn and hugged Emma, too, softer and quieter, but with an identical smile of welcome. "I'm glad to see you," she said. "Natalia's been driving me nuts. At last I have someone normal around."

"Hey!" Natalia fake-punched her sister in the arm, pretending to pout. "I'm the most normal person you know. And Emma is *mine.*"

"Whatever." Zoe rolled her eyes, but she squeezed Emma's hand.

Emma smiled at both of them, taking in the changes since she'd last seen them in December. Zoe had cut her dark hair into a sleek bob, but Emma had seen that when they'd Skyped. The summer sun had brought out Natalia's freckles, and her bathing suit showed through her shirt in damp pink patches. Zoe was cool and clean in a white T-shirt and mint-green shorts, looking as crisp as if they had just come out of her drawer.

The twins were identical, but hardly anyone ever mixed them up. Natalia's long hair flew everywhere, whipping across her face, part of it yanked back into a careless ponytail. Zoe's swung neatly to just below her chin. Natalia's eyes sparkled and her mouth was never still—she was always laughing loudly or talking as fast as she thought, words spilling from her lips. Zoe was more reserved, quieter. Her smiles were just as warm, but smaller, and she kept a lot of her thoughts private. When Natalia was talking, Zoe was sketching and drawing instead, or watching everyone with an amused expression on her face.

When they were all together, Emma liked to think of herself as the balance between her cousins. She was quieter and less reckless than Natalia, but less watchful and reserved than Zoe.

Natalia grabbed her arm. "Come on," she said. "Let's go down to the beach. I've got a plan."

"It's a very *wet* plan," Zoe said, a smile lurking at the corners of her mouth.

Riley finally made it across the lawn and sniffed at Emma's fingers before licking them. She petted him. "Good boy, good boy," she said. "Did you miss me?"

"Riley can help with the plan," said Natalia as she tugged Emma away from the car.

"Hang on, girls," said Emma's mom. She hugged Natalia and Zoe hello. "Emma has to go say hi to her grandmother and everybody before she can do anything else."

"Plus, the cookout is the first thing on my list," Emma said brightly. Even though she was dying to know what Natalia's plan was, she was starving.

"Oh, you and your lists," Natalia said, and sighed.

"I like the lists," Zoe said. "It's very orderly. Very Emma."

The cookout was just as Emma had pictured it. Grandma Stephenson and Emma's aunts and uncles fussed over her, talking about how they couldn't believe she and Zoe and Natalia had all graduated from fifth grade and were ready to move on to middle school. To them, it seemed like the girls had been babies just a few days ago.

Abuelita hugged and kissed her and told her how

beautiful she was and how much she had grown, before loading Emma's plate with homemade tamales. Abuelita had grown up in Mexico, and she always said traditional dishes from there were the best.

"Try a brownie," Natalia said, handing her a plate.

"Huh," said Emma, poking at it. There were weird purplish bumps sticking out of the top.

"You look so suspicious," Zoe said. "I promise it's good. We added dried blueberries and butterscotch chips this time."

"Interesting," Emma said. That explained the purple bumps, anyway. She took a cautious bite. "Good," she said, chewing. She wasn't *entirely* sure about the blueberries, but they weren't terrible.

Aunt Alison called Zoe and Natalia away to help in the kitchen for a moment, and Emma took her loaded plate and sat next to her grandmother. Grandma Stephenson seemed thinner and smaller than she had at Christmas, but her blue eyes were as sharp as ever.

"Hello, Granddaughter," Grandma Stephenson said, solemnly, looking her over.

"Hello, Grandmother," Emma answered, in the same formal voice. They grinned at each other, and Emma felt something relax inside herself—Grandma hadn't changed, not really.

Emma told Grandma Stephenson about how the school year had been (she and her best friend, Amelia, had both been forwards on the school soccer team, and they'd won most of their games) and about her plans for the rest of the summer (camp, mostly, and she had a long summer reading list for starting sixth grade). Grandma had taught English at the high school in town for forty years, and she had a lot of opinions on the books Emma was supposed to read: "Oh, *The Giver*, that's a classic" or "I think you'll like *Because of Winn-Dixie*; it's got a dog in it."

It was all really normal, and Emma felt the little anxious tightness in her stomach—the worry that Grandma Stephenson would have changed since her fall—relax. Despite the heavy gold-topped cane hooked over the arm of her chair, she was still Grandma.

The conversation paused. "Um, Grandma?" Emma began awkwardly. "Are you feeling okay? Since you had to move in here?" She poked hard with her fork at Aunt Bonnie's potato salad, not looking at Grandma, in case she was upset.

Grandma Stephenson laughed a little, and Emma looked up. "I don't think *had to* is quite the right phrase. I'm glad to spend time with Alison and her family. Although it is a little crowded." She took a sip of her lemonade. "And Abuelita was wonderful about looking after me while I was recovering. If she wasn't a registered nurse, I probably would have had to stay in the hospital a lot longer than I did. I'd probably *still* be there, doing physical therapy and fighting with my doctor."

"But don't you miss Seaview House?" Emma asked, and then blushed. Of course Grandma did, and it wasn't fair to bring it up, not when she wasn't well enough to live alone anymore. "I'm sorry," she said. "It's just that— well, you grew up there, and so did your parents, and I always loved the house so much. And I liked the garden especially."

Emma thought back to last summer. Set in terraces going down the hill down to the beach, the garden at Seaview House was filled with sweet-smelling flowers: trailing honeysuckle and wisteria on one level, roses on another, bright yellow black-eyed Susan on another. Standing on the lawn of the house, all you could see were flowers, all the way down to the bay.

"The garden, of course. I always loved it, too," Grandma Stephenson said, looking a little dreamy. "I was married in the garden, you know. We set up an arch on the path along the lawn, and were married under it. It was a sunny, hot day, and all the roses were in bloom. The scent was everywhere."

Emma could picture it, because she'd been at Seaview House on hot summer days when the smell of roses hung, heavy and sweet, all through the air. It made you sleepy, until the cool salt breeze came off the bay and woke you up. The rose-and-sea scent made everything seem about twice as romantic as it was in real life.

"What's going to happen to the house?" she asked suddenly. She hadn't really thought about it—she'd just thought about Grandma not being *in* the house anymore. Her uncles and aunts had their own houses, and she couldn't imagine them leaving and moving into the huge, rambling house on the top of the hill. But it couldn't just sit empty forever, either. Was Grandma really okay with not going back? "Are you going to sell it?"

That terrible, tight, almost-crying feeling was in Emma's throat again, but she blinked back her tears. It wouldn't be fair for *her* to cry, not when it was *Grandma* who might be losing her house. "It's just hard to think of it not being ours anymore," she whispered. "I don't like things changing."

Grandma gave her a long look, her blue eyes sharp, and then patted Emma's hand. "Not all changes are for the worse, you know," she said.

"I know," Emma agreed, and said the next bit in a singsong reciting voice: "The important thing is that we're all together now."

"Well, it's true," Grandma said. "Just look at us all."

Emma looked around. Her dad and the uncles had all congregated by the grill and were talking as smoke rose in lazy spirals toward the blue sky. Mateo and Tomás ran across the lawn, screaming with excitement, as Riley determinedly followed along behind, panting. Abuelita and Aunt Bonnie were sharing a plate of cookies at the picnic table, their heads bent together in conversation. Natalia came out of the kitchen carrying a plate of ribs—"Watch it!" Zoe said behind her, her hands full of plates—piled so high they wobbled and almost fell. From the kitchen, Aunt Alison said something Emma couldn't hear and laughed.

"We're all still here, whatever house we're in," Grandma said firmly. "I'll always love Seaview House, but family is what matters."

"I guess so," Emma said, looking down at her hands as she fiddled with her food. She couldn't help feeling as if she was losing something important. Seaview House *was* almost like family—it had held her mother's family, the Stephensons, for generations. It was their past—and *her* past, too. She couldn't imagine it not being part of her future.

Chapter Two

While Emma ate, Natalia had been bouncing back and forth between Emma and Zoe, eager to drag Emma down to the beach to show off the new game she'd invented. Finally, once everyone was stuffed full of brownies and watermelon, the three cousins crossed the road and climbed down the grassy bank to the edge of the beach. Natalia and Zoe's little brothers tagged along after them. Riley came, too, lagging behind as he creakily hauled himself down the slope, his bushy tail waving. Emma waited for him, burying her hand in the thick ruff of hair at the nape of his neck as they walked down toward the shore together.

This stretch of the beach, north of where the tourists stayed and only accessible from the backyards of family houses, was almost deserted, with only an older couple in the distance collecting shells down by the water.

"Ta-da!" Natalia said.

On a tarp lay what looked like hundreds of brightly colored . . .

"Water balloons?" Emma asked.

"Not just any water balloons," Natalia corrected. "The Most Amazing Water Balloon Game Ever."

"We were filling balloons all yesterday and this morning," Zoe added, sighing. "Sometimes I think Natalia's actually five." Natalia stuck out her tongue at Zoe.

"We helped," six-year-old Tomás added, and their four-year-old brother, Mateo, nodded enthusiastically. "We get to play, too."

"See the Hula-Hoops?" Natalia asked, pointing at three red hoops placed to make the points of a large triangle on the beach, weighed down here and there by piles of sand to keep them from blowing away. "If you throw a balloon from the starting line here and get it in one of the side hoops, that's five points. The middle one, farther away, is ten. If you get your first balloon in, you can throw again for twice as many points, but you have to throw it backward over your shoulder without peeking, and other people can try to catch the balloon in midair. If they catch it without it breaking or hitting the ground, they get all the points you have so far."

"Sounds fun," Emma said, flexing her fingers. She was good at throwing and catching; she'd played softball for a couple of summers.

"Sounds like we're all going to get soaked," Zoe said. "And like we'll spend all evening picking up bits of water balloon off the beach." Natalia made another face at her, and she added, "But fun, too, yeah."

"I've been practicing catching balloons," Natalia said with a smirk. "Fear me, because I am going to be the champion."

"You can go first, Emma," Tomás offered generously. "Since you just got here."

Emma picked up a pale blue balloon and hoisted it in her hand, getting used to the weight. It was cold and squishy. She swung her arm experimentally, squinting at the hoops. She could probably win the game, she thought, no matter whether Natalia had been practicing or not.

Emma threw the balloon and it flew in a perfect arc, landing with a splash right in the middle of the center hoop. Her cousins cheered, and Riley barked with excitement, his shaggy tail whipping the air.

"Ten points!" Tomás shouted.

"Wow," Mateo said, hopping up and down. "That was really, really good."

"The challenge is the next part," Natalia said, handing her another balloon. "Turn around, and no peeking. If you get it in, you get another twenty points."

Her back to the hoops, Emma was sure that her muscles remembered the exact force she had used to throw the balloon. She could get it in again. She focused and threw the balloon back over her shoulder.

Swinging around to look, she was just in time to see Natalia leap for the balloon and almost catch it, knocking the balloon from its course just enough to send it shooting right into Zoe's face. It burst, soaking her head with water.

"Oh!" Zoe said, gasping. Her eyes narrowed and she grabbed for a balloon, starting toward her sister. "It is *on*."

Emma watched, knotting her fingers together nervously as Zoe ran after Natalia, pelting her with balloons. *Are they playing? Or is she really mad?* Zoe's mouth was in a tight line beneath the streams of water running down her face from her hair.

"Oh no you don't!" Natalia yelled, catching one of the balloons that Zoe had thrown at her and tossing it back. She was laughing, though.

Zoe tossed the balloon at Natalia, but lightly, so it landed on the beach and splattered Natalia's legs, not her face. "Come on," she said, pushing her wet bangs out of her face. "It's your turn."

Gradually, most of the adults came down to the beach and started tossing water balloons as well.

But Emma's mom and Aunt Alison had wandered farther down the beach and were talking intently, leaning in toward each other as if they had a secret. Emma wondered what it was.

But as her mother followed Aunt Alison to the throwing line, Emma decided it was all in her mind. The sun was shining and everyone was laughing. Everything was just as a summer afternoon in Waverly should be.

As the sun got lower behind the houses, they finally declared a winner. Uncle Luis held his arms high in triumph: "The champion! Fifty points!"

Then, as Zoe had predicted, they all had to clean up the beach.

"Blargh," said Emma, carefully picking a scrap of red rubber from a mass of seaweed at the edge of the water. "How did a balloon even get all the way over here?"

"There was a lot of out-of-bounds chasing," Zoe said seriously.

"I think we've pretty much got it all now, though," Natalia said. Satisfied with the cleanliness of the beach, the rest of the family was starting to head back toward the house, Aunt Alison carrying Mateo. Riley followed them, his bushy tail waving. Shadows were spreading, and Emma shivered as a brisk breeze sprang up from the water.

It was almost the end of the first day at Waverly, Emma realized. Only six more to go before they'd have to leave again. *I wish we could stay longer*, she thought again.

Emma's mom turned and called back, "Are you girls coming up?"

"We'll be up soon!" Natalia shouted back.

They watched as the others crossed the beach and climbed the grassy hill toward the house. Emma sat down and dug her feet into the still-warm sand.

"What should we do?" she asked carefully. She knew what she wanted to do, but it had been six months since she'd seen her cousins. What if they'd outgrown the pact?

"Cousin pact, duh," said Natalia cheerfully, and Zoe nodded.

They'd started the pact the summer when they were seven, just old enough to have private games. Already at that point they'd been inseparable when the family was all together. The pact had been changed and refined as they got older, but the most important parts had stayed the same.

They stood and walked together to the edge of the water, gentle cool waves lapping at their toes. Each of them bent down and took a handful of sand.

"Our days together slide like sand through our fingers," Natalia said solemnly. They opened their fists and the damp sand oozed through their fingers, leaving their hands gritty.

"The tides go in and the tides go out," Zoe said, looking out at the horizon, "but we stay the same."

"Not just cousins and sisters, but best friends," Emma

said, and her cousins chimed in on the last word as they reached out to join hands. "Forever."

~◌~

Back at the house, it was almost fully dark. The family gathered in the backyard, where Grandma Stephenson, seated in a sturdy lawn chair, was handing out sparklers.

"Be careful, children. Don't rush Grandma," Abuelita scolded lovingly.

"I'm scared to hold it when it's lit. You hold mine," Mateo said, pushing his sparkler at Tomás.

Lightning bugs were rising from the grass, flashing secret codes at each other. Emma took the sparkler her grandmother handed her and sat cross-legged on the lawn, waiting for Uncle Luis to get out a lighter and light them all.

"Look," Zoe said, sitting down on one side of Emma. "You can see Orion's Belt." She pointed, her finger tracing a line of stars. The stars were bright against the deep darkness of the sky. As Emma tipped her head back, she felt almost as if she was looking down into the night, as if she could fall and fall into the depths of the nighttime sky.

"The stars are way brighter here than in Seattle," she told Zoe. "Because there aren't so many lights and buildings."

"I'd like to come to Seattle again," Zoe said. "Remember when we stayed with you guys two years ago? You're so lucky. I'd love to live in a city."

"It's better here," Emma told her. Seattle was cool, but Emma couldn't imagine not wanting to live in Waverly, right by the bay and surrounded by everyone who loved you. Zoe shrugged, looking unconvinced.

"Hey!" Natalia plopped down on Emma's other side. Her sparkler was fizzing and shining and she touched it to first Zoe's, then Emma's. Emma jerked back reflexively as hers burst into sparks, and both her cousins giggled.

The sparklers smelled like smoke and, beyond that, Emma could smell the salt and sand of the bay. Crickets chirped somewhere out in the darkness, and grass tickled the back of Emma's legs. Natalia leaned against her, her side warm against Emma's. An almost-full moon was shining in the sky above them. *"I see the moon, and the moon sees me,"* Zoe sang softly beside her, leaning back on her elbows.

A whole week of Waverly stretched out in front of her, feeling like both a long time and not long enough. Emma wasn't going to think about having to leave, not yet.

A cool breeze gently lifted Emma's hair. Right now, everything was perfect. Emma wished the moment could last forever.

Chapter Three

I don't want to leave, Emma thought. She was floating on her back in the bay, gentle waves lifting her in a steady rhythm. Gulls screeched overhead in the blue afternoon sky. She could hear Mateo squealing as Zoe tossed him in the waves and the more distant voice of Natalia helping Tomás to build a sand castle on the beach.

It had been a really good week, but it had flown by. The three girls had swum almost every day, and Uncle Dean had taken them out on his boat a couple of times. They'd had a bonfire on the beach and eaten s'mores until their hands and faces were sticky. Emma's dad had driven her and the twins up to spend a day at an amusement park, where Natalia had dared the others to ride all the scariest rides and Zoe had treated them all to ice cream and Emma had won a stuffed dog by throwing darts at balloons. All the time, Emma had felt the minutes ticking by, counting down to when their vacation would be over and she'd have to say good-bye.

They'd had so much fun, but they hadn't gotten to do everything on Emma's list. They hadn't had time to knit, for instance. There was never enough time in Waverly for Emma to do everything she wanted.

Almost over kept going through her head. Early tomorrow morning, she would be on a plane back home.

Squeezing her eyes closed, she tried to think of what they should do this last night:

1. Family board games?

That might be fun—if everyone wanted to play, and no one fought, and they didn't get stuck playing the baby games Mateo and Tomás would want.

2. Beauty Night?

Natalia had suggested giving each other makeovers and painting each other's nails one night—she had a collection of nail polishes in shades ranging from bright white to forest green to pastel blue to black, but they hadn't gotten around to it.

3. Cooking?

They'd talked about making a whole dinner for the family. Zoe claimed she knew how to make lasagna, but they'd never gotten around to that, either.

⤷⤶

With a sigh, Emma brought her legs down and stood upright, water streaming down her back from her hair. *It's over*, she thought. *There just wasn't time for everything, and I've got to accept that.* Zoe splashed over to her, holding Mateo's hand. "Want to head in?" she asked. "I think Mateo's lips are turning blue."

Natalia looked up as they waded into shore. She and Tomás had abandoned their sand castle, and she was patting warm sand over and around her brother's feet. "Okay, pull your foot out *carefully*," she instructed. "Look! A turtle house. Tonight a little turtle will come and live in it and maybe we'll see him come out in the morning." Tomás giggled.

Emma's chest ached with sadness. "I won't have time to come down to the beach in the morning," she said, her voice wobbling.

Zoe wrapped an arm around her shoulders. "Don't worry," she said, her brown eyes warm with sympathy. "There won't really be a turtle. It's just a game."

Natalia rolled her eyes. "You're such a pill," she said. "Tomás and I believe the turtle is real." She smiled at Emma as Tomás nodded fiercely. "Anyway, Emma's not sad about that. She's just going to miss us."

"Well, duh," Zoe said. She bumped her hip into Emma's. "We'll miss you, too, Em. But it won't be long till Christmas."

Emma didn't say anything. It felt really real now, that everything was ending. If she tried to talk, she thought she might cry.

Up at Zoe and Natalia's house, all the adults had already gathered for another big family dinner, this one a good-bye. Two long picnic tables set end to end in the backyard were spread with newspapers. By the time the kids had changed out of their swimsuits, plates of steamed crabs sat on each table, flanked by baskets of rolls and bowls of coleslaw and potato salad.

"Oh, yum," Emma said, sitting down next to Natalia and reaching for the nearest crab plate. You couldn't get sweet blue crabs like these in Seattle, they were a Maryland thing, so Aunt Alison and Uncle Luis made sure to schedule a crab feast every year when Emma and her parents were visiting. The little aching part inside her reminded her: *The last night, the last night.* But she pushed it away. She would enjoy *now.* Zoe sat down on her other side and grabbed a roll.

After everyone had enjoyed their fill of delicious crab, Aunt Alison, Abuelita, and Emma's mom brought out a tray of cookies and fruit. Aunt Alison and Emma's mom stayed standing at the end of the table, looking around at the assembled family.

"Before you start dessert," her mother said, "I— Alison and I—have something important to tell you." The sisters took each other's hands and smiled, eyes shining.

Zoe nudged Emma and raised an eyebrow question- ingly, but Emma shrugged.

"Brian and I miss all of you so much when we're home in Seattle," Emma's mom went on, and her dad nodded. "And our jobs are so high-stress, we don't see Emma enough. We feel like we're missing out on what's really important in life."

"Amy and I have had a dream for a long time," Aunt Alison chimed in. "Since we were girls, really. And now we can realize this dream in a place that was so important to us growing up, and which is so important now to the whole family."

Natalia's hand gripped Emma's knee hard suddenly, as if she'd realized, or suspected, something, but Emma frowned. She still didn't have a clue what their mothers were talking about.

"Anyway," her mom went on, "Alison and I have always planned that we would someday open a bed-and-breakfast together. And when we married Brian and Luis, they became part of that dream. We wanted to use our skills to make people happy, to make a place that was beautiful and welcoming. And I wanted to be able to spend more time with Emma and with all of you."

Emma's heart was pounding. Did her mom mean . . .

Emma's mom looked at Grandma Stephenson. "Mom has agreed to sell us half of Seaview House," Emma's mother announced. "Brian and Emma and I are going to leave Seattle and come to live in Waverly, and open a bed-and-breakfast in the old family house with Alison and Luis. And Brian and Emma and I will live there, and Grandma will come and live with us. While Emma's at camp this summer, Brian and I will get us ready to move. We'll all come back out here before school starts."

Grandma Stephenson smiled around at the assembled family. "It's taken me a while to make this decision. I wasn't sure I wanted to let anyone take over my house, or if I could cope with the change of letting strangers come and stay in it. I wanted everything to stay the way it was." She leaned forward, and now she was looking directly at Emma, her blue eyes bright. "Emma helped me realize that sometimes change is necessary. It's important that Seaview House stay in the family." She smiled. "I want my grandchildren to be able to have *their* weddings in the garden someday."

The world swung dizzyingly around Emma. She

couldn't breathe. *Everything* was going to change, and it had happened so fast. Zoe had tight hold of her arm, and Natalia was gripping her knee still, but both seemed temporarily stunned into silence.

All around, her family was exclaiming and asking questions. Emma's mom caught her eye and came over, kneeling on the grass next to the picnic table.

"I'm sorry I couldn't tell you before," she said quietly. "But I didn't want to get your hopes up. Grandma didn't make up her mind to let us have the house until today. Are you happy?"

Emma took a deep breath, the world steadying. Was she happy? What a ridiculous question. "We're moving to Waverly. We're going to *live* here! This is what I always wanted!" She could hardly believe it.

"This is amazing," Natalia said in Emma's ear, and Zoe bounced in her seat.

Emma smiled around at everyone, feeling light-headed with joy. Waverly had always been home in a way nowhere else was, a place where generations of her mother's family—her family—had grown up. She'd always wanted more time here, more time with her family and especially with her cousins, her two best friends in the whole world. And now, like a huge, unexpected gift, she was going to get what she wanted.

A warm glow was building in her chest. "I can't wait," she said. "This is going to be perfect."

⁓

Six weeks later, Emma's best friend in Seattle, Amelia, dropped her head down on the restaurant table and wailed, "This is *terrible*!"

In a few days, Emma and her mother were going to move to Waverly. Two weeks after that, school would start. Her dad would move out to Waverly as soon as he had hired and trained a new chef at Harvest Moon.

Emma loved coming to Harvest Moon, with its rich food smells and the way that the waitresses always treated her like she was special, and she loved bringing her friends here. Her dad had invited her to bring her best friend, Amelia, for a special good-bye lunch. Now, though, she was almost regretting it.

"What are we going to do without you?" Amelia asked, raising her head to look at Emma accusingly. "The soccer team's going to lose all their games, for one thing."

Emma almost felt bad that she didn't feel *worse* about leaving. She was going to miss her friend, of course. But there was this happy little bubble inside her that kept reminding her: She was getting what she'd always wanted.

"No, you're not," Emma reassured Amelia. "You'll get someone really good in." Not that it felt great to think of someone else taking Emma's spot as star forward on their team—she'd worked so hard to get there, and they'd gotten to the point where they won most of their games.

"And what about school?" Amelia continued. "This is the year we get to take a ferry out and go camping in the San Juan Islands."

Emma's heart sank a little. The weeklong sixth-grade camping trip to the San Juan Islands was something she'd looked forward to for ages. She hadn't really thought about the fact that it was finally time and she wasn't going to be there. Did Waverly Middle School's sixth-graders get to do anything special? And, even if they did, would it be as much fun for her, if she was the new girl? *Not really new*, she reassured herself. *I'll have Zoe and Natalia.* But, even so, she couldn't help feeling just a little anxious. Beneath the table, she twisted her fingers together, trying not to worry.

Julia, the nicest of Harvest Moon's waitresses, came over and began putting plates down on the table. "How are you doing?" she asked, as she placed Emma's fried chicken and waffles in front of her.

"Good, thank you." Emma untangled her fingers and smiled at Julia, reaching for her fork—she loved the cinnamon her dad added to the crispy waffles in this dish.

"Your dad has a special surprise dessert made up for you girls." Julia sighed and shook her head. "We're going to miss you all coming in here on the weekends. You were just finishing third grade that first summer. Remember your ninth birthday party?"

Emma nodded. "It was a lot of fun." Her dad had gotten them the private party room in the back, and they'd played games and eaten a whole tower of cupcakes in every flavor from chocolate with raspberry frosting to creamy butter pecan.

She'd had so many celebrations at Harvest Moon—not just birthdays, but family dinners and last-day-of-school parties.

And now she never would again.

As Julia walked away, Emma turned back to see Amelia smile wanly.

"It's more than just the team and school and every-thing," she said softly. "I'm just going to miss you."

"Yeah," said Emma, swallowing. Her throat was suddenly dry, and her eyes ached like she might cry. "I'm going to miss you, too." And it wasn't just Amelia. Now that she was moving to Waverly, now that she was getting what she had always wanted, it suddenly felt like she was leaving a lot of good things behind.

She shut her eyes for a moment and thought fiercely to herself: *I'm not going to worry about this. It's going to be amazing.*

Chapter Four

This is definitely not amazing.

Emma shifted uncomfortably on the air mattress on her cousins' floor, trying not to make too much noise. There was a weird lump under it. As she turned over, the mattress suddenly squeaked loudly and then went flat in one spot so that her shoulder hit the floor.

"Shh!" Zoe said irritably, mostly asleep, and pulled her pillow over her head.

Emma sighed and shifted around again to get off the flat spot. She definitely wasn't going back to sleep, she thought grumpily. Was it too early to get up?

The renovations at Seaview House had started in the summer, while Emma and her mother were still in Seattle. The roof repairs were done, but, as Emma's mom had explained, what you really needed for a bed-and-breakfast was a lot of bathrooms and a professional kitchen, which were still being installed. And so the plumbing and the kitchen were currently unusable, which meant Emma and her family couldn't move in.

Worse, her dad wasn't even with them. He was still in Seattle, because Harvest Moon didn't have a new chef to take over for him yet.

Emma's mom was staying up the road in Uncle Dean and Aunt Bonnie's guest room, but everyone had thought Emma would have more fun with her cousins. She'd spent the last week sleeping on the floor of Zoe and Natalia's room. It was pretty fun. Mostly. Especially at first.

They'd had a campout on the beach behind the house, just the three of them in a tent on the soft sand. They'd caught up on their summers and painted each other's nails, and Emma had shown both her cousins how to make perfect folded origami boxes the way one of her cabin mates at camp had taught her.

It was great to be with Zoe and Natalia again, Emma thought, but she definitely wasn't getting enough sleep and, after a whole week, Emma was *tired*. On top of the uncomfortable air mattress, Natalia snored. And Mateo still had to be woken up and walked to the bathroom in the middle of the night. Every time Aunt Alison or

Uncle Luis went into his and Tomás's room to get him up, Emma heard them in the hall and woke up, too.

There was definitely something digging into her back, it wasn't just an air mattress lump. Emma sat up and wiggled her hand under the half-deflated air mattress. She just managed to touch something smooth and cool with the ends of her fingers. *Metal?* She slipped off the side of the bed and sat on the floor to get her arm underneath. Scraping her fingers against the carpet, she dragged it out. A tiny toy car. *Tomás and Mateo.* They were cute, but their toys got everywhere, and it was no use telling them to stay out.

Emma wasn't used to having little kids around. At her own home, things had always stayed where she put them, and strange objects that didn't belong to her never wandered into her room. *There are too many people in this house*, she thought, then felt disloyal.

She sighed and sat up. Even with the car out from under the mattress, she was still too uncomfortable to go back to sleep. Peering at Zoe's alarm clock, she saw that it was only seven o'clock.

Emma got up and looked at her cousins. Zoe seemed to have gone back to sleep with her head under her pillow and her arms and legs sprawled across her bed, but Natalia's eyes fluttered open and she looked up at Emma, yawning. "What's up?" she asked.

"I'm hungry," Emma whispered. "Want to get something to eat?"

"Sure." Natalia bounced out of bed. Emma looked at Zoe, but Natalia grabbed her arm and pulled her toward the door. "Ugh, don't wake her," Natalia said. "She's such a grump in the mornings; it'll be more fun if it's just us."

"Okay," Emma said, but she looked back at Zoe's sleeping face. She didn't *want* to wake her—it was true that Zoe was definitely not a morning person. But it felt weird that Natalia didn't want her with them. Emma didn't think Natalia was right—things weren't more fun without Zoe, they were more fun with the three of them together.

Down in the kitchen, it was warm and sunny and smelled of cinnamon. Abuelita was standing at the counter, rolling out a rectangle of dough, while Grandma Stephenson sipped coffee at the kitchen table.

"You're up early," she said approvingly.

"Good morning," Emma said to them both. "Yeah, I woke up earlier than usual." She didn't add how uncomfortable she had been, or that Natalia had accidentally stepped on her face in the middle of the night when she'd gotten up to go to the bathroom, and that it had taken her hours to doze off again.

"Yum, cinnamon rolls," Natalia said, flopping down in a chair at the table. "We can eat them all before everyone else gets up." Grandma raised an eyebrow at her, and Natalia shrugged. "I'm sorry to have to say it, but once you have five kids in a house, it's survival of the fittest."

Five kids was a lot for one house. Emma had thought it herself, but now that Natalia said it, she felt her shoulders tense. She was the extra one, after all. Did Natalia not want her here?

Abuelita blew her a kiss. "My hands are sticky, or I'd hug you good morning, dear. Would you like some juice?"

"I'll get it for her." Grandma Stephenson, supporting herself on her cane, began to get to her feet.

"Nonsense, you don't want to put unnecessary strain on your hip. I'll get it." Abuelita put down the bowl and began to wash her hands at the kitchen sink.

"I am perfectly capable—" Grandma was on her feet now.

"I'll get myself the juice," Emma said hastily. She opened the refrigerator and took out a carton of orange juice as Grandma sat down and Abuelita turned her attention back to the rolls. "Can I help with those?"

"Sure," Abuelita said. "Get out about a third of a cup of butter and melt it. We'll brush it over the top and then sprinkle on the sugar and cinnamon. Should we put in raisins or walnuts?"

"Why not both?" Emma asked, with a smile at Natalia. She popped the butter into the microwave to melt, and Abuelita laughed.

"I'll get the walnuts," Natalia said, getting up. "The added protein makes the rolls practically health food."

"Uh-huh," Emma said. "Delicious sugary health food."

"Speaking of sugar, I can mix the glaze at least," Grandma told Abuelita. "If you insist, I'll even let you get out the ingredients and I'll stir it up sitting right in this chair."

"No, no, you just take it easy." Abuelita jokingly wagged a finger at Grandma Stephenson, and Emma turned around from taking the butter back out of the microwave to see Grandma roll her eyes up to the heavens. "I like taking care of everyone. Now, Emma, take this brush and spread the butter all over the top of the dough."

As Emma began brushing the dough, she looked at her grandmother again. Grandma Stephenson had her lips pressed tightly together, as if she was reminding herself to keep her temper. "Well," she said evenly, after a few minutes. "If I'm not allowed to do anything—"

"The most important part of any recovery is rest," Abuelita said cheerfully.

"*If* I'm not allowed to do anything useful, I'd love to hear how my granddaughter is feeling about this move. I imagine Waverly is a big change after Seattle, Emma."

"It must have been hard to say good-bye to all your friends," Abuelita added.

Emma glanced up quickly to find two pairs of sympathetic eyes, one clear blue and one warm brown, fixed on her. She stared back down at the dough, carefully covering it with a layer of sugar and cinnamon. It *had* been hard, that was true.

The thing was, Emma had always wanted to be part of the family's life in Waverly. She had always wanted to be able to be with Natalia and Zoe, her best friend-cousins.

But.

But it had been really *hard* to say good-bye to her friends, and they had all cried and promised to keep in touch, but Emma knew it wouldn't be the same between them. And it had been hard to leave their nice little town house on Queen Anne Hill in Seattle—and her father— behind, and who knew when he would be able to come . . . Emma realized that her eyes were filling with tears, and she swallowed hard and reached for the raisins.

"She *loves* it," Natalia said decidedly, leaning on the counter to grab a handful of raisins. "Emma couldn't wait to come here." She said it like she could answer this question just as well as Emma could.

"Well," Emma said slowly, concentrating on placing the raisins evenly across the dough. She didn't want to hurt Natalia's feelings, and it wasn't like she *wasn't* glad to be in Waverly. "I *am* really happy to be here, mostly. I've always wanted to live—"

Quick footsteps on the stairs interrupted her.

"Rolls!" Tomás shouted delightedly. "Can I squinch them up?" He pushed at Emma so he could reach the end of the dough and try to start rolling it. Her juice glass fell to the floor and shattered. "Oh, no! No! I'm sorry!" Tears started to run down his chubby cheeks.

"It's okay." Emma hugged him. "It was an accident." Tomás sniffed and wiped his eyes on the shoulder of her pajamas.

"Nobody move until I clean that up," Abuelita said, going for a broom.

There was a shout from upstairs. "Mommy! Mommy!" and Aunt Alison answered, her footsteps padding down the hall.

Zoe came into the kitchen, her usually smooth hair wild and unbrushed. "I *wondered* where you were. You could have woken me," she said. "Oh my gosh, cinnamon rolls. Tomás and Mateo are going to be on a sugar rush all morning."

"Don't step another foot," Abuelita warned, sweeping.

Uncle Luis wandered in, his eyes half-closed, and fumbled at the coffee maker. "Careful," Grandma Stephenson warned him. "There's still some glass on the floor."

The moment to tell Abuelita and Grandma what she was feeling had passed, Emma decided. Maybe she'd talk to them later. But not in front of Zoe and Natalia.

They were both just so *sure* that everything about this move was great for Emma.

There wasn't a chance to talk about anything much to anyone at all over breakfast; everyone was grabbing cinnamon rolls and bacon and fruit and talking over and around each other.

I'm just not used to this kind of thing, Emma thought. She was used to a quiet bagel at a table with usually just her mom, since her dad worked late hours at the restaurant and then slept in. Four adults and five kids at the same table was a lot louder than Emma's regular mornings.

After breakfast was cleared away, Uncle Luis announced that he was taking all the kids to get their school supplies.

"Oh," Emma said, startled. "My mom usually takes me." She and her mom would take a whole morning on it, picking out folders and notebooks and pencils, and then have lunch at a restaurant together. It was calm and orderly, and Emma found herself twisting the bottom of her T-shirt, feeling worried at this change, even though there was no real reason to be. It was just another thing that was different, was all.

"It'll be more fun with us," Natalia said confidently.

"Your mom and I have a meeting with the contractors this morning," Aunt Alison said, and Emma nodded. After all, she figured, Uncle Luis was a high school teacher, so he was probably especially good at picking school supplies.

At the school supply store, though, Uncle Luis just set them loose to pick what they needed. Mateo, who was starting nursery school and only needed things like crayons and safety scissors, took up all his attention because they had to be the exact *right* crayons and scissors and everything needed to be inspected, slowly and carefully. Tomás tagged along with them, grabbing his own first-grade supplies and dumping them in the cart with only a quick glance.

Emma was used to looking at everything with her mom, and, despite being surrounded by her cousins (and about a million other kids and parents getting set for school), she suddenly felt a little bit lonely.

"I've got the list," Zoe said. "I *know* you want to carry it, though, Emma." Emma nodded and took the sheet of paper. She did feel better, seeing exactly what she needed, carefully laid out for her. They were all in the same class, so they all needed the same supplies.

As Emma checked things off the list, Zoe efficiently steered them from one aisle to the next, and Natalia kept wandering off and coming back with pencil cases that unzipped to show mouths full of zipper teeth or notebooks with pictures of kittens in funny poses. After a while Emma started to have a good time.

"Ooh," said Natalia, as they got to the far end of the store. "Look at how cute that backpack is." It was light blue, with a darker blue and teal butterfly spread across it.

"Pretty," Emma agreed.

"Let's all get them," Natalia suggested. "We can be a team. Team Butterfly Girls."

"Okay." Emma liked the idea. She'd start the new school already visibly belonging, one of a matched set of three.

"I am *definitely* not getting matching backpacks," Zoe said firmly. "I'm getting that pink-and-white one."

Emma felt a little hurt. Still, it would be fun to match Natalia. And of course, Natalia and Zoe were *already* a matched set, even without the backpacks.

"Fine, evil twin, be that way." Natalia made a face at her sister and hooked two of the butterfly backpacks into the cart.

"That's the whole list," Emma said, checking off *backpack or satchel.* "We are officially ready for sixth grade."

They found Uncle Luis and the little kids. Mateo had opened his box of crayons and was carefully counting to make sure there were twenty-four, but he kept losing track and starting back over at one. Tomás was whining and complaining that his feet hurt, and Uncle Luis looked as if he wished vacation was already over and he was safely back to teaching algebra to ninth-graders.

"Can we go get ice cream?" Natalia asked. "Emma hasn't been to Sweet Jane's yet."

"Sure," Uncle Luis said glumly. "If we're not outside to meet you in half an hour, tell your mother I've run away."

Zoe patted him on the back as they left.

Sweet Jane's was at the other end of Waverly's main street and sold all kinds of sweets: cookies and brownies and little hand-dipped chocolates in the shapes of flowers and suns. But mostly they sold ice cream from a long glass case that seemed to have every flavor you could imagine.

"Black raspberry's my favorite," Zoe said, pointing to one with swirls of different shades of purple.

Natalia had to try all the weirdest flavors before she ordered anything: Cinnamon Bear, which was bright red and had tiny bear-shaped graham crackers in it; Crispy Crunchy, which was marshmallow ice cream with chocolate chips and chunks of rice cereal treats mixed in; Ultimate Darkness, which was just chocolate with chocolate chips and chocolate-covered nuts and chocolate-covered pretzels. The girl behind the counter just laughed and passed over more tiny spoonfuls to try.

Emma was pretty sure she wanted mint chocolate chip, but she tried the Ultimate Darkness, too, and the Dulce de Leche caramel, just in case those were better.

"Jalapeño?" Natalia said thoughtfully. "Do you dare me?"

"I absolutely don't dare you," Emma said. "That sounds awful."

"I dare you," Zoe said. "Go ahead."

The shop door burst open and two girls about their

age came in, and Natalia squealed and ran over to them, the jalapeño ice cream forgotten.

"Hi, Bridget, hi, Caitlin," Zoe said, sounding polite but not especially interested.

"This is my cousin Emma," Natalia told the girls, and they said hi to Emma, too, then went on giggling with Natalia.

Emma started to feel a little left out, standing in the ice-cream parlor while Natalia and her friends laughed about something Emma couldn't hear. Zoe had gone back over to the ice cream and was waiting for the girl behind the counter to scoop her up a cone of the black raspberry.

"I guess they're really good friends of Natalia's?" Emma asked, wandering back over to her.

"Natalia's friends with everybody. She's a social but-terfly," Zoe said, rolling her eyes. "Bridget and Caitlin are okay, but Natalia and I don't really hang out with the same people at school. Usually we're in different classes, but they put us in the same class this year."

"Oh," Emma said, surprised. Didn't Zoe *want* to be in the same class as Emma and Natalia? If Zoe and Natalia didn't stick together at school, who was Emma going to be with? She had pictured the three of them always together, the way they had been on holidays and vacations. She addressed the girl behind the counter. "Mint chocolate chip in a sugar cone, please."

Natalia hugged her friends good-bye when she saw that Zoe and Emma were ordering. She came over and ordered a double scoop of Cinnamon Bear and Ultimate Darkness.

"That seems like a gross combination," Zoe commented, and Natalia widened her eyes indignantly.

"Ish delicioush," she said, mouth full.

"Let's get ice cream for Uncle Luis and the boys," Emma suggested, and they ordered a scoop of chocolate for each of the boys and rum raisin for Uncle Luis. Each carrying two cones, they stepped back out into the sunshine.

The mint chocolate chip was delicious, creamy and sweet, and Emma decided not to worry about school yet. Zoe and Natalia were her friends and her family and it would all be fine. They still had two days to go before school would begin.

Chapter Five

* Blue skirt

* Black leggings

* Light blue shirt with the fox on it

Emma, sitting on the air mattress, bit her lip, thinking. Was that too much blue? The skirt and the shirt were different shades, but still . . . she didn't want to look blah and all one color on the first day of school tomorrow. She wanted the other kids to *like* her, to look at her and be, like, "Hey, she looks like she'd be nice to know."

She pressed her hands against her stomach, which was beginning to squirm with anxiety. She'd thought that it wouldn't matter meeting all these strange kids, because she'd have Zoe and Natalia. But it sounded like they didn't even stick together at school. Would they want to hang out with Emma? Who would she go with if they went in different directions?

She sighed and crossed out the blue outfit. There must be something better she could wear.

She had that red-and-white-striped skirt, but wouldn't that be too Fourth of July–looking with the blue shirt? Wait, the red-and-white skirt was still packed in a box, waiting to move into Seaview House, Emma realized. She wasn't even sure what she had to wear tomorrow other than the old summer clothes she'd been wearing for the last couple of weeks.

She sighed and crumpled up her list. There was nothing *wrong* with the clothes in her suitcase. She was just tired of them.

Natalia was sprawled across her bed, reading, while Zoe was drawing at her desk. But at the sound of the crumpling paper, they both looked up.

"What's the matter?" Zoe asked.

"I'm sick of living out of suitcases," Emma said. She gritted her teeth. *This would be a really stupid thing to cry about*. But she could picture herself, dressed in faded, worn summer clothes, standing all alone at school as Zoe and Natalia ran off with different friends. Each of the three of them separate instead of the tight team of three Emma had imagined.

Zoe and Natalia exchanged a look, and Natalia got up and came to sit on the air mattress next to Emma, criss-crossing her legs. The air mattress gave a protesting squeak and sank a little lower.

"But isn't it really fun living out of suitcases?" Natalia tried. "You can pretend you're camping?" Emma and Zoe both stared at her, and Natalia grinned sheepishly. "Okay, maybe not. But it's not forever." She knocked her shoulder against Emma's gently. "And we like getting to live with you."

Zoe picked up the crumpled list from where Emma had dropped it and uncrumpled it. "You need an outfit for school tomorrow," she said, reading it.

"I realized those clothes are all packed," Emma admitted.

Natalia bounced up, and the air mattress vibrated wildly. "You can borrow something of mine!" she said. She flung open her closet, and Emma frowned. It was hard to see what Natalia had because everything was jammed in together, but there were lots of really bright colors, wild patterns, and T-shirts with funny pictures or sayings on them. "How about a T-shirt that says *Brightest Witch of Her Year* on it?" Natalia asked. "Or you could wear this dress with the stars." The dress sparkled in the sunshine coming through the window, each glittery star sending out a ray of light.

All Natalia's clothes are perfect, Emma thought. Perfect for Natalia. They looked just like her.

Some of them Emma would love to borrow, sometime. But Emma didn't want to start a new school dressed up as Natalia. She wanted to feel like herself.

"Ugh, she doesn't want to wear *your* clothes, Natalia," Zoe said.

"What's that supposed to mean?" Natalia asked indignantly. "Emma dresses more like me than she does like you."

"So not true," Zoe said loftily. "Emma has natural style." She turned to Emma. "I know what you need." She opened her own closet, which looked just as neat and organized as Zoe herself—as different from Natalia's closet as Zoe and Natalia were from each other. Shirts were separate from pants, were separate from skirts, were separate from dresses. Everything faced the same way on its hanger, and—Emma tilted her head, squinting—it kind of looked like the different sections of clothing were then sorted by color.

"Wow," Emma said.

"You haven't seen this before?" Natalia asked. She was still frowning about Zoe's criticism of her wardrobe, and her tone was a little grouchy. "Doesn't it make her look just a *little* bit crazy?"

"I like being able to find anything as soon as I want it," Zoe said calmly. "Anyway, my mom bought me this dress and I never wore it. It's nice, but it didn't feel like me. I think it feels like *you*."

Zoe pulled a dress out of her closet. It was soft and knee-length, with thick blue-and-white stripes, and pockets in the front. Emma could imagine herself starting school in it tomorrow.

She hesitated. The dress was perfect, but she didn't want to hurt Natalia's feelings.

"Oh, go ahead and take it," Natalia said. "I know you want to. And Zoe's right, it'll look nice on you."

"Thanks," she said to Zoe. "Are you sure?"

"Of course." Zoe shrugged. "It matches your eyes; it's meant to be yours."

"It's cute," Natalia said reluctantly. "Kind of preppy maybe, but less boring than most of the stuff in Zoe's closet."

Emma hugged the dress to her, feeling lighter and happier. Maybe she was living out of a suitcase still, but at least she had something new for tomorrow. And it seemed like the twins weren't annoyed with each other anymore.

The front door banged, and Emma heard her mother and Aunt Alison's voices downstairs.

"Girls!" her mother called. "Are you ready to go?"

"Go where?" Emma asked.

Natalia grimaced apologetically. "Oh, shoot, we forgot to tell you. They called while you were in the shower to see if we wanted to go check out what they've done to Seaview House."

"Great!" Maybe this meant that they were a lot closer to moving in than Emma had thought. With any luck, she wouldn't be living out of a suitcase for much longer.

Seaview House was a *mess*. There was no furniture in the downstairs rooms, and the floor was gritty with tracked-in dirt. A hole gaped in one wall, showing a tangle of pipes.

"I thought the construction was going to be almost done by now," Emma said, feeling faint. What were they *doing* to Seaview House?

"Where's all the furniture?" Natalia asked, looking around. Zoe said nothing, running her fingers over a windowsill and then scowling at the plaster dust now coating her fingers.

"It *is* almost done," Emma's mom told her. "Once the bedrooms down here are finished and it's painted, and the new kitchen is in, we'll furnish the rooms."

All three girls looked around doubtfully, and Aunt Alison laughed. "You'll see that all this chaos will have been worth it when it's done. There's even one room down here that's already finished." She turned down a short hall and opened a door that Emma remembered as leading into a musty-smelling dark-paneled study that no one had used much since Grandad Stephenson had died, way back when Emma was little.

Emma gasped. The room had been totally transformed. It was bright and airy now, the dark paneling gone, the walls white and blue instead. Flowered curtains hung at the windows, and the furniture was familiar—a big bed made of dark wood with high posts on each corner and a matching chest of drawers, a dainty dressing table, and a small secretary desk with a top that folded down.

Zoe looked around. "This is stuff from Grandma Stephenson's bedroom," she said. "What's it doing down here?"

"This is going to be her new room," Aunt Alison said. "It'll be hard for her to get upstairs to her old room, so this is all fixed up for her."

The girls exchanged glances. The room was nice, but it seemed so final to change Grandma's room.

Natalia asked what they were all thinking. "So, Grandma isn't going to get better enough to go back to her old room upstairs?"

"Well," Aunt Alison said, "it'll be easier for her to get around every day if she's on the ground floor. It takes her a while to climb stairs."

Emma looked around. The windows of Grandma Stephenson's new bedroom looked out onto the terraced garden. When they were open, the scents of the flowers and the bay would blow right in. "It's a nice room," she said. "Has Grandma seen it? She'll like being right over the garden."

Her mother slung her arm around Emma's shoulders. "Of course she's seen it," she said with a smile. "Who do you think told us how she wanted all the furniture arranged?"

"Come on upstairs," Aunt Alison said. "We have more to show you."

"Onward with the tour!" Emma's mom said.

Upstairs, it was more of the same—new bathrooms being put in, pipes sticking out of the walls in some of them, the sharp smell of paint and the grit of plaster dust everywhere.

This isn't going to be finished for ages, Emma thought glumly.

Emma's mom wiggled her eyebrows at Emma. "Want to see *your* room next?"

My room? When Emma had stayed with Grandma during visits, she'd slept in a guest room that they'd already passed: It had had its worn pink wallpaper scraped off, and looked just like all the other half-finished rooms.

"We thought we'd have more privacy if we lived at the top of the house," her mom explained. She pushed on an almost invisible door. It had been covered with wall-paper to match the hallway exactly. Emma's mom led them up the hidden staircase that ran from the base-ment to the attic, with narrow landings outside the entrance to each floor.

The secret staircase hadn't changed at all, Emma saw with relief. It was narrow and dark and beautifully familiar. When they were seven, she and Natalia and Zoe had spent most of one Christmas afternoon racing their new dolls down the stairs on sleds made of card-board. It had been very satisfying to see them zoom down from one landing to the next.

Natalia and Zoe ran ahead up the stairs, their mom hurrying after them, but Emma lingered a little, enjoy-ing the secret stairs. They were musty and creaky and a little bit spooky, but in a good way.

Emma's mom stayed with her, linking their arms together, and Emma leaned against her. "How are you doing?" Emma's mom asked. "I've been so busy that it feels like we haven't really talked for a while. Are you okay at your aunt and uncle's house? Are you excited about school tomorrow?"

Emma thought about it. She wasn't really *excited* about school, or she was, but there was a deep anxious pit in her stomach whenever she thought about it. And living at Natalia and Zoe's family's house was fine, but she missed her mom and dad.

"Nothing's really wrong," she said slowly. "It's just hard because it's different, you know?"

Her dad never cooked at the restaurant on the night before school started; that was a night for him and Emma. If they were back in Seattle, she knew, her dad would be taking her out tonight for their special father-daughter back-to-school pizza night. They'd go to the pizza parlor downtown that had huge, greasy pies and share one with pineapple, olives, and mushrooms on it, which they both liked and her mom thought was a disgusting combination.

And when they got home, her mom would make them all cocoa and they would slump down on the couch together and watch something funny and dumb on TV until Emma was full and laughing and didn't have any room inside to worry about the next day.

But tonight she'd be here, and her dad was back in Seattle for at least another week. Emma wondered what Zoe and Natalia's family did the night before school started.

"I mean, everybody's being really nice to me," she told her mom. It was true, even if Zoe and Natalia weren't always nice to each other. "I don't want you to think I'm not happy to be here."

"Oh, Emma," her mom said, squeezing her arm affectionately. "Please don't worry about the fact that you're worrying. It's natural to be nervous about a new school. But Natalia and Zoe will help you, and pretty soon it'll feel like you've always been here."

"I guess so," Emma said. She decided not to mention that Zoe and Natalia might not both stick with her at school, not if they didn't stick together with each other. Instead, she turned the corners of her mouth up in a smile. "I think I'm all set for school," she said, making sure she sounded cheerful. "Zoe and Natalia helped me pick out the perfect outfit."

"Good. And remember, I'm only a phone call away."

Her mom squeezed her arm again and looked up to the top of the stairs, where Natalia was bouncing impatiently on the attic landing.

"Emma, hurry up," she called. "My mom won't let us go in ahead of you. She says it's your new place, so we have to wait."

When Emma and her mom pushed open the hidden door to the attic, Emma had to stop for a moment and stare.

Seaview House had a large attic. It had expanded as various new parts of the house had been built, over several generations, so now there were a couple of different big rooms. The floor wasn't level between them and you had to step up or down as you crossed from one wing of the house to the other. The whole thing was filled with generations of put-aside stuff, from the front layer of things like Christmas ornaments and beach toys and the badminton set that got pulled out regularly to tons of old furniture to boxes labeled things like MAUDE'S WEDDING DRESS (whoever Maude was) and a ton of trunks and boxes that weren't labeled at all. It was an amazing place to explore on a rainy day.

Now the piles and piles of stuff had been moved so that

the rambling rooms on the left side of the staircase were more crowded than ever, and on the right side of the staircase was a new white wall and a red-painted door.

"Go on," Emma's mom said, smiling, when Emma hesitated, so Emma turned the knob and opened the door.

Inside, the scratched attic floorboards had been polished so that the dark wood shone, and the walls were freshly painted white. A tiny gleaming kitchen led into a small bright living room. A half-open door showed yet another new bathroom (but finished this time, it looked like, with plumbing and everything). On the far side of the living room were two more doors, and Emma's mom pointed to the one on the left. "That one's going to be yours."

Emma turned the knob. The room had a slightly slanting ceiling, low enough that she could reach up and touch it on the side where the windows were. She crossed the room to look out. The windows themselves, like Grandma Stephenson's, looked out over the gardens toward the water, but Emma's were high enough that she had a good view of white sailboats scudding across the big blue expanse of the bay. The other side of the room was lined with white built-in bookcases. There was no furniture, but the room was bright and sunny, and Emma could picture herself here.

"Cool!" Natalia said approvingly, and Zoe nodded.

"Once the house is ready, we can get our own stuff out of storage," her mom said. "And if there's anything you want from the attic for your room, you can have it, as long as Grandma says it's okay."

There were fancy rugs rolled up in the attic, Emma knew. And a painting she'd found once when she was poking around. It showed a thin, green-eyed girl, who was probably an ancestor, dressed for a dance.

"You could take one of those old trunks and make a window seat," Natalia said.

"Could I?" Emma asked. A window seat would be cool; she could sit and read or watch the sailboats. When thunderstorms came, she could watch lightning cracking over the bay.

"Definitely," Natalia said. "And you can keep stuff inside it. Just make sure to take one of those big, old, tough ones and you can put cushions on top and it'll be perfect."

"I think that would probably work," Aunt Alison said. "If you're set here for a while, I'm going to go look at the progress the contractors have made with the kitchen downstairs."

She headed out and Emma's mom looked like she was about to follow her, but then her phone rang. She looked down and said, "Excuse me, girls," and went out into the new living room.

"You're lucky," Zoe said.

"Am I?" Emma asked. "I mean, it's a nice room, but your room is nice, too."

Natalia rolled her eyes. "Our room is okay, but we have to share it. According to Zoe, sharing a room with me is total torture. That's why she says you're lucky."

"I just want you to pick up your stuff sometimes." Zoe was using a slow, patient voice, as if Natalia was a little kid, and Emma wasn't surprised when Natalia flared up.

"Maybe if you weren't so compulsive about every-thing being in the right place," Natalia snapped.

Zoe, looking hurt, was opening her mouth to reply when Emma broke in.

"Please don't fight, you guys." She hated it when they started squabbling. They hadn't always been like this, had they? Emma's memories of vacations spent with her cousins were all about the three of them having fun together. Peacefully.

Zoe sighed. "What I was *going* to say, before Natalia interrupted, was that you're lucky that you get to start from the beginning and make this room exactly how you want it to be. We've been in our room since we were babies. Our mom and dad chose all the furniture, and our beds are in the same place they decided our cribs would go before we were even born."

"True." Natalia agreed. "There's no room for anything new. And you get to pick from all the old stuff in the attic, plus your own stuff. You could probably furnish, like, ten bedrooms with everything stored up here."

"Make a list, Emma," Zoe said, grinning. "I've got some paper. And I can sketch out plans for where everything might go."

The three of them sat in a circle on the floor of the empty room and discussed the possibilities. Zoe and Natalia, Emma noticed, at first talked to her more than to each other, but after a bit, seemed to forget to ignore each other.

"You could hang fabric on the walls," Natalia said. "Like tapestries. It would be cool."

"Emma likes things clean and simple," Zoe argued. "What about leaving the walls white and putting up white Christmas tree lights?"

Out in the other room, Emma could hear her mother talking on the phone. Not the words, but she registered in the back of her mind that her mom sounded, not angry exactly, but exasperated.

"What about a *hammock*?" Natalia was saying when Emma's mom came back in. "No, listen, it would be great, and then during the day you could roll it up and you'd have more room."

"Like on a pirate ship," Emma said, distracted. Her mom held the phone out to her.

"It's your dad," she said.

After they'd said hello, Emma's dad asked, "What's like a pirate ship?"

"Oh, Natalia thinks I should sleep in a hammock," Emma said. When her dad laughed, something that had felt knotted up inside Emma relaxed. She missed him, and he was far away, but her dad sounded happy and just like he always did.

"I'm sorry I can't be with you for our special last dinner before school starts," he said. "How're you holding up?"

"Okay," Emma said. "How are things with you?" She didn't want him to worry about her, since he had so much else going on.

Her dad told her about what he'd been doing—mostly working—and about helping in the search for another chef to replace him. "We interviewed one who seemed great," he said. "He'd cooked at restaurants all over the country, and we all liked him. Then we started calling his references, and none of them had ever heard of him. Nothing he'd told us was true."

"Maybe he was a *ghost*," Emma said in a deep spooky voice. *"We had a cook by that name once, but he died fifty years ago on this very night."*

Her dad laughed, but then his voice softened and got serious. "So the search for my replacement is taking longer than we thought it would. I won't be home next week after all."

Emma's heart sank. She hadn't realized how much she'd been counting on seeing her dad until he said he wasn't coming.

"I can't leave them in the lurch," her dad said. "But I'll be out there as soon as I can. I hope you understand."

"I do," Emma assured him. And she did—of course her dad wanted to help find the right chef to take his old job. The restaurant, and the people who worked there, were important to him. But suddenly the idea of fixing up her new bedroom was less exciting.

"I wish I was there with you, but I know you'll have a great first day of school," her dad said.

"I wish you were here, too," Emma said. As she hung up the phone, she hoped that her dad was right about tomorrow.

Chapter Six

When Uncle Dean picked them up the next morning, the sails on the *Bonnie Jane* (named after Aunt Bonnie, of course) were hanging limp. The outboard motor was rumbling quietly as he waited for them at the end of the dock.

"Ready for the first day of school?" he asked, hopping out to help the girls into the boat.

Emma smoothed down the blue-and-white-striped dress nervously. She didn't feel ready, but she took Uncle Dean's hand anyway and let him steady her as she hopped onto the *Bonnie Jane*.

"Ugh, school," said Natalia, making a face. "Can't we just go for a sail instead?"

"Nope, first-day-of-school sail has to involve going to school," Uncle Dean said, picking her up and swinging her down into the boat.

Until Zoe and Natalia told her last night, Emma hadn't known that this sailboat trip was how the new school year always started for them. Uncle Dean turned the boat out into the bay, cutting the motor and raising the sail, and Emma settled back into her seat as the sail caught the wind and the boat surged forward.

The breeze lifted Emma's hair, and she looked out across water gleaming in the early morning sunshine. A seagull screeched overhead, and Uncle Dean turned the rudder, catching the wind and speeding lightly forward through the waves.

Emma relaxed and tipped her face up toward the sun. Whatever happened today, this was a million times better than riding the school bus on the first day of school.

They had time for only a short sail before the girls had to get to class. Uncle Dean tied up at the dock of a friend who lived only a block from the school, and the girls climbed out, straightening their clothes and hitching their backpacks up onto their shoulders.

"Thanks, Uncle Dean," Emma said, and the twins echoed her. They waved good-bye as he headed back out into the bay, and they turned toward school.

"There it is," Natalia said, waving one hand at the brick school. "We've got three more years there, so resign yourself to the agony."

The sun was still shining brightly, but Emma felt cold.

She'd seen the school before—it was hard to miss; Waverly wasn't that big—and it was perfectly normal looking. Three stories of red brick with big windows and a playground in the back, it held all the grades from kindergarten through eighth grade—the town wasn't big enough for a separate middle school.

But now the building seemed to loom over her, its windows dark and ominous. And full of strangers. *Deep breaths*, Emma coached herself, sucking in air. *I can stay calm.*

"Nine months of prison before summer comes again," Natalia said mournfully.

"Oh, it's not that bad," Zoe said. "Stop trying to scare her. It's fine, Emma. It's just a school."

Emma knew Zoe was right, but the perfectly normal redbrick school still seemed sinister, like it was casting a shadow over the nice sunny sailing morning she'd had. Zoe and Natalia didn't understand, she knew. They had always been here; they didn't have to meet everyone for the first time now. The deep breaths helped the sick, panicky feeling to lessen, but she was still scared.

As they got closer to the building, they saw more and more kids—little ones being walked in by their moms, older ones climbing off school buses or out of cars, others walking by themselves or in groups—all heading for school. One kindergartner was clinging to her mom's legs, wailing, "No! No! I don't want to go!"

I know how you feel, kid. Emma wondered how Zoe and Natalia would react if she tried the same thing.

"Natalia!" A group of girls ran to catch up with them. Natalia's friend Caitlin, whom Emma had met at the ice-cream parlor, was one of them.

"Hi," Emma said to her.

"Oh, hi," Caitlin said shortly, eyeing her, and turned away, starting to talk excitedly to Natalia. It wasn't rude, exactly, but something in Caitlin's look made Emma suddenly aware that she'd just gotten off a boat. She was probably all flushed. She put up a hand to feel her hair and realized it was frizzing out in all directions.

"Hey, Emma," Zoe said. "These are my friends Louise and Ava."

They both looked sleek and put together in the same

way Zoe did. Ava's dark hair was divided into many tiny braids and pulled into a side ponytail. Louise wore a crisp white sundress that popped against her brown skin. They said hi and Emma said hi back, but she couldn't focus, suddenly so aware of how messy and frazzled she must look. Natalia's hair, she saw, was windblown, but Natalia wouldn't care. Zoe's hair had fallen back neatly around her face. Emma felt hot suddenly, as if everyone was watching her. *Deep breaths*, she told herself again.

"Do you have a comb?" Emma asked Zoe suddenly, interrupting something Ava was saying about their teacher. "Sorry," she told her. "Excuse me."

Zoe looked Emma over and grinned. "Yeah, come on," she said, pulling her inside and to the girls' bathroom.

Emma looked into the mirror and groaned. Her hair was as bad as she had thought.

"What's up?" Zoe said, taking a comb out of her backpack and handing it to Emma. "You're not usually so freaked out."

"I'm not usually starting a brand-new school," Emma said, a little sharply.

"It's going to be fine," Zoe said.

"You've been saying that to me all morning," Emma snapped, exasperated.

"Well, it's true. Here," Zoe said, taking back the comb, and she pushed Emma's hair behind her ears and dug in her backpack again, bringing out a small silver barrette. "There," she said, fastening it. "You look great."

I do look better, Emma thought. The tightness in her chest was receding. Zoe was good with her hands and good at making things look right, whether she was drawing a bird, decorating a room, or fixing hair. Emma's reflection was more polished already, her hair smoothly framing her face. "Thanks," she said. "I'll try to relax."

"Don't relax too much right now, or we'll be late for class," Zoe said, and led the way back into the hall.

When they walked into the classroom, Natalia was already there, sitting at a desk near the front and swinging her legs. "Hey, Emma, sit here," she said, patting the desk next to her. "I saved you a seat."

Emma hesitated and glanced at Zoe, but Zoe was already sliding into a desk closer to the back of the room, beside Louise. They had said they didn't hang out all the time at school, but she felt weirdly disloyal to Zoe as she took the desk next to Natalia.

If I sit with Natalia, am I choosing her over Zoe? Is Zoe going to be mad? But Zoe wasn't even looking at Emma.

The room was filling with students. *These are the kids I'll be with all year,* Emma thought, looking around. Most people were talking about their summers at the top of their lungs. One girl with a face-framing braid was reading quietly; a boy was staring out the window.

"Good morning, class," the teacher at the front of the room said loudly, and everyone got quiet. "Most of you already know me, but in case you don't, I'm Mr. Thomas, and I'll be your homeroom teacher this year."

Mr. Thomas was maybe a little younger than Emma's parents, with brown hair and rounded silver glasses. He was kind of short for a grown-up, and his chin stuck out in a long point. He looked okay, Emma thought.

"We have a new student joining us this year," he said cheerfully. "Emma Blake, why don't you stand up and tell us a little about yourself."

Emma froze, instantly changing her mind about Mr.

Thomas. He was *not* okay. She'd seen teachers do this to new kids on TV shows, but she'd never heard of it happening in real life before. Her hands were sweating, and she awkwardly wiped them on the skirt of her dress.

Mr. Thomas nodded at her encouragingly. "Come on, Emma. On your feet."

Slowly, she got up. Was this really necessary? Natalia was smiling at her. "Go, Emma!" she mouthed.

She didn't know what to say.

Her mouth was dry, and she could feel everyone staring at her. "Okay," she said, staring at her shoes. Her voice came out husky and quiet, barely more than a whisper. She licked her lips nervously.

"Speak up, please, Emma," Mr. Thomas said cheerfully. "And look up at the class."

Emma dragged her gaze back up to look at everyone. They were all looking back at her, almost thirty pairs of eyes, staring right at her. The nervous twist in her stomach was so strong it made her feel like she might throw up.

"I'm Emma Blake," she said, speaking louder this time. Her voice sounded funny to her own ears. She didn't know what else to say, and the silence stretched longer and longer. Someone giggled. *I can't throw up*, Emma thought. *Not here. Deep breaths.*

"Where are you from, Emma?" Mr. Thomas asked.

"Seattle," she said, and swallowed hard.

"Seattle! A terrific city," Mr. Thomas said. "What's your favorite subject, Emma?"

"English, I guess," Emma told him, and sat down quickly, before he could ask her anything else. She felt flushed and sweaty. Why did she have to be so *weird* and panicky? It was just school.

"Well, welcome, Emma," Mr. Thomas said. "Speaking of English, let's move right along into class." He reached for a stack of books on his desk. "The first book we're going to read this year is *Catherine, Called Birdy*. I think you'll like it." He began handing the books out to the front row to pass back.

"Ugh," Natalia said, looking at the girl in medieval clothes on the front. "Historical fiction."

"No, it's really good," Emma said quietly, feeling more confident now that she had the safety of a desk in front of her, and now that she could think about the book instead of about herself. She'd taken this out of the library last year. "It's funny. Her father wants to marry her off, but she keeps getting rid of her suitors."

"Do the boys have to read this, too? This is a girl book," one of the boys in the back of the room complained, but Mr. Thomas ignored him and smiled at Emma.

"You've read it!" he said. "And you liked it! I can't wait to hear what you have to say in the class discussions."

"I learned a lot about medieval history from it," Emma said, feeling shy but pleased with her teacher's praise.

"And that's the other reason we're reading the book," Mr. Thomas said to the class. "We'll be starting with the medieval period in history class, and we can talk about what's accurate in this book and what's not." He started to write an assignment on the board, and Emma pulled out her notebook to copy it down, the class's attention no longer on her.

By the time lunch came around, Emma was feeling better about school. Mr. Thomas taught the sixth grade both English and history, and he seemed like he was going to be interesting. They'd had science and gym in the morning, too. The science teacher seemed nice, and she'd said they were going to study marine life and take trips out into the Chesapeake Bay to learn about the ecosystem right around them. And they were starting with volleyball in gym, which Emma knew she was good at. Smacking the ball over the net was always satisfying.

She'd only gotten lost once, and it wasn't long before Zoe had come and found her, and Natalia had saved her a seat in all their classes. *Maybe sixth grade is going to be okay*, Emma thought hopefully as she followed Natalia into the cafeteria.

Zoe and her friends were already sitting at a table near the cafeteria entrance. Zoe looked up as they came in and smiled at Emma, sliding over to make room for her. Emma hesitated, looking after Natalia, who had continued on into the cafeteria.

"Emma, come on!" she called impatiently. Emma looked back and forth between her cousins, feeling awkward.

Zoe shrugged at her. "It's okay if you want to sit with Natalia." Emma followed Natalia.

"What I want to know," Natalia said, plopping down at a table, "is *why* we have to take gym *every* day. I read that you're supposed to give your muscles a rest and only work out every other day."

"I think that's for stuff like weight lifting, not playing games," Emma said, sitting next to her and pulling out her packed lunch. She looked back at Zoe. She had always thought that, if she lived in Waverly, she and Natalia and Zoe would be one tight group, the way they were on vacation. What did it mean if they weren't together? It felt weird to be with one of her cousins and not the other. Did Zoe mind? She had said it was okay, but maybe Emma should have sat down with her instead. She'd been with Natalia all morning. "How come you and Zoe don't sit together?"

"We told you, we don't hang out that much at school," Natalia said, biting into her sandwich. "We're so different. Plus, we just have different friends."

Natalia, Emma thought, had a *lot* of friends. The table was crowded with them. Natalia was in the middle of everything, talking to about five different people. Caitlin, on Emma's other side, leaned past her. "Hey, Natalia," she said. "Did you see Dan's face when Ms. Patel said no calculators?" Emma didn't know who Dan was. She realized she was twisting her hands together nervously and made herself stop.

"Hey," the girl across the table from her said. Emma thought her name was Vivian. "Do you want to trade desserts? My mom packed me these chocolate chip muffins I don't like."

"Sure," Emma said, handing over her cookies. The muffins looked good, but Emma didn't feel hungry.

It was so loud in here, and Emma couldn't remember everyone's names. She needed a break.

Pushing away from the table, Emma said to Vivian, "I'll be right back."

Going over to Zoe's table, she stood awkwardly next to it for a moment. What if Zoe didn't want her? "Hey," she said.

"Oh, hi," Zoe said. She moved over and let Emma sit down. "You okay?"

"Yeah, why?" Emma said, automatically smoothing her hair.

"I don't know, you just look kind of worried," Zoe said. Her friends, whose names Emma had forgotten, nodded.

"No," Emma said. "Not really. I didn't want you to think I was avoiding you. I just—Natalia wanted me to sit with her."

"You know how Natalia likes to take things over," Zoe said. She didn't seem mad, though. One of her friends—the blonde one—started getting up and Zoe smiled apologetically. "We were going to go to the art room since we're finished eating. It's too loud in here. You want to come?"

"Um." Emma looked back to see if Natalia was looking for her, but Natalia seemed totally absorbed in her conversation. "I haven't finished lunch yet." She was tempted, though. The art room was probably quieter than the cafeteria, and less crowded.

But Zoe was already getting to her feet. "Okay," she said. "See you in math, then."

"Bye." Even though Zoe had invited her to go with them, Emma felt a little abandoned as she watched her walk away with her friends. She wasn't ready to go back to Natalia's table yet, either—it was too crowded. Emma chewed on her lip, then made herself stop. *Everything's fine,* she reminded herself.

When she got back to Natalia's table, her seat was gone. Caitlin had slid across the bench into Emma's place next to Natalia, sliding her lunch over, too, so that there was no space for Emma. Emma's own lunch box was closed and more toward the middle of the table. Vivian, chewing on Emma's cookies and listening to Caitlin, didn't look up when Emma hesitated behind her.

Emma stood there for a minute, waiting for Caitlin to move. Caitlin looked up but didn't say anything. There was a tense moment where they just stared at each other.

Natalia didn't seem to notice. "Hey, Emma," she said. "We were just talking about whether to join theater club this fall. You should totally join, too! They're probably going to do *The Wizard of Oz* this year."

Caitlin frowned. Emma had the distinct impression that she would *not* be happy if Emma decided to join *The Wizard of Oz*.

Could Emma really ask Caitlin to move and give her seat back? It didn't seem like something to make a big deal out of. She grabbed her lunch box and took another seat, a little farther down the table.

"Hi," the girl next to her now said. "You're Natalia's cousin, right?"

"Uh-huh," said Emma, and tried to smile at her instead of staring down the table at Natalia and Caitlin talking about theater. Natalia didn't seem to have noticed that Emma had moved.

Losing her seat didn't really matter, but there was something about the whole thing that made Emma's chest ache. It felt like maybe, despite being part of a family who'd lived here for practically forever, she didn't fit in here so well after all.

Chapter Seven

Emma flopped down on the school bus seat and leaned back, closing her eyes. "This has been the most exhausting week of my life," she said, as the bus's engine began to rumble.

Natalia bounced next to her in the seat, and Emma opened her eyes again. "It was great, though, right? You finally got to meet everybody! It was awesome!"

Her eyes were wide and hopeful. *No,* Emma sort of wanted to say. *It wasn't awesome. Your friend Caitlin seems like she hates me for some reason, and I wish you and Zoe and I were all together like we are at home.*

Looking at Natalia's enthusiasm, though, Emma chose not to say any of that. Instead, she said: "Yeah, but I'm just worn out. It's *hard* being the new kid."

She could see the back of Zoe's head a few rows ahead

of them. She and Louise were deep in conversation. She never sat with them on the bus.

When the bus pulled up to their stop, though, Zoe cheerfully joined them in climbing off, and Tomás hopped out of his front seat with the other first-graders.

"How was school today?" Emma asked Tomás. Tomás was the most enthusiastic first-grader ever, she'd discovered. Every day he had something exciting to announce.

Now his eyes widened and he turned to them excitedly. "Ms. DeVico said that I get to be attendance monitor next week!" He waited for their reaction to this big announcement.

"Good job, Tomás," Natalia said.

"What's attendance monitor?" Emma asked, and Tomás stared at her in disbelief.

"You don't have *attendance monitor*? It means that next week I get to go down to the office every morning with a list of everybody who's missing from class."

"A very important job," Zoe said.

"Oh. Good for you, Tomás," Emma agreed. Tomás

strutted down the sidewalk in front of them, proud of himself.

"Do you guys want to go to the movies tonight?" Natalia asked. "Caitlin and Bridget and some of those people are going."

"Hmm," Emma said noncommittally. "I'm kind of tired." What she really wanted to do was call Amelia or one of her other friends back home. If she could get a minute alone.

"Mommy!" Tomás shouted, pushing the front door open. "We're home!"

"We're in the kitchen," Aunt Alison called back.

Dropping her backpack in the hall, Emma followed her cousins to the kitchen.

"Hey, everybody!" Emma's mom was pulling a pan out of the oven. "Special snack time!"

"It smells amazing in here," Emma said. The air smelled like hot butter, maple syrup, and cinnamon. Emma's stomach growled.

"We thought we would try out a few recipes on you guys," Aunt Alison explained. Mateo, who got home an hour before the older kids, was already sitting at the table, drinking apple juice. Grandma Stephenson was sitting with him, stirring something in a mixing bowl, while Abuelita poured tall glasses of milk for the other kids.

"It's time to work on the breakfast part of B and B!" Emma's mom said joyfully. She put the hot baking pan down on the counter. It was full of what looked like French toast and fruit. "We have a bunch of recipes to try before we open."

"Oh, yeah," Emma said, her mouth watering. "You know what? We should put Dad's special crepes on the menu." Her dad made these thin, crispy crepes and filled them with a fruit compote of raspberries and peaches; Emma had never tasted anything so good.

"Well, honey," her mom said, picking up a knife and cutting into the French toast stuff, maybe a little more fiercely than necessary, "we'll definitely put those on the menu, but I'm not sure when your dad is going to get here. So we're going to need some other choices."

Emma looked at her mom warily. "But I thought Dad was coming soon."

Her mom shrugged a jerky, angry shrug. "I don't know. He doesn't know. It depends on the restaurant."

"Oh." Emma sat down at the table, feeling shaky. She hadn't realized she was counting on her dad arriving soon, but now she realized she had been assuming he'd be home any day.

She took a bite of the French toast. It was sweet but thick in her mouth. Her throat felt tight, and she had some trouble swallowing it. "It's okay," she said. "Kind of dry maybe?"

Natalia sat down next to her, giving Emma a sympathetic nudge, and took the fork out of her hand. "Let me try," she said, biting into the French toast. "It's good. Is there any maple syrup?"

Grandma passed her a pitcher, and Natalia doused Emma's plate.

"Hey, get your own plate," Emma said indignantly.

"Yum, but this is a lot of carbs and sugar," Zoe said. "Don't you think we need some protein?"

"You are *such* a buzzkill," Natalia said, shaking her head and stealing a syrup-soaked blackberry off Emma's plate. Emma smacked her hand.

"Get your own. Mom, would you give Natalia a plate? She keeps stealing mine."

"There's two quiches cooling on the counter over here if you want something less sweet, Zoe," Aunt Alison said. "One's mushroom and Swiss, and the other's sundried tomato and feta, but they have to cool for at least another fifteen minutes or they'll fall apart when I cut into them."

"Gross," Tomás said. "Can we have pancakes?"

"I could make bacon," Zoe said. "That's a protein."

"And *super* healthy," Natalia said jokingly, digging into the plate of French toast Emma's mom handed her. Zoe made a face at her and started looking for bacon in the refrigerator. Mateo knocked over his juice and Tomás laughed.

Emma rested her head on one hand and poked at a strawberry as the volume steadily rose in the kitchen. The French toast was good, but she was just so tired. Grandma Stephenson was looking at her, and, as their eyes met, they shared a secret smile. Emma was pretty sure that Grandma got as worn out by being around everyone all the time as she did.

Aunt Alison brought a row of tall glasses filled with layers of fruit, granola, and yogurt out of the refrigerator. "Try these," she said, setting one in front of everyone except for Zoe, who was now heating her bacon on the stove. "Yogurt parfait." She sat down at the foot of the table.

"Not bad," Abuelita said. "I like a hot breakfast myself, but you'll get some people in who only want cereals and yogurts and things. Smart to cater to them, too."

Emma took a bite. The yogurt was sweet and creamy, and she liked the crunch of the granola.

Aunt Alison smiled at her. "So, how was your first week of school?"

"It was okay," Emma said. "Some of the kids are nice, some not so nice."

"What?" Natalia's head jerked up, and she stared at Emma indignantly. "Who's not being nice to you?"

"Well . . ." Emma hesitated. She didn't want to get into an argument about Natalia's friend.

Before she could decide how to answer, Zoe broke in. "She means Caitlin," she said. She turned to face them, the bacon sizzling in the pan behind her.

"Caitlin?" Natalia frowned, confused. "What's *Caitlin* done?"

"It's not like . . ." Emma didn't know how to explain it. "She's just not that friendly."

Natalia shook her head. "I haven't noticed anything," she said defensively.

"You know how Caitlin is," Zoe said. "She gives Emma these *looks* all the time. She's just jealous, Emma."

Natalia frowned stubbornly. "I would have noticed. Are you just trying to make Emma hate my friends?"

Zoe glared at her. "I'm not making Emma do anything."

"Girls . . ." Aunt Alison said, sounding tired.

Natalia opened her mouth to say something else, and Emma interrupted her. "Please don't fight, you guys," she said. "Caitlin's fine. Don't worry about it." The last thing she wanted was for the twins to fight about *her.*

The bacon hissed, and then suddenly the pan was full of fire. Zoe shrieked and ran toward the sink.

"No!" Emma's mom shouted. "No water!" She grabbed a lid from the drying rack and slammed it down on top of the pan.

The fire sizzled and went out. The kitchen was silent

and full of smoke. After a moment, the smoke alarm began to beep, loud and insistent. Mateo burst into tears.

"Never put water on a grease fire," Emma's mom said, breathing hard. "It'll just spread it. You have to cut off the air to the fire."

"Wow," Zoe said, staring at the stove. "I'm sorry. I got distracted."

"Typical," Natalia said, clearly trying to continue their fight.

"Not really," Zoe told her coolly. "More like something *you'd* do."

Aunt Alison had picked Mateo up to comfort him, while Abuelita pulled over a step stool and climbed up, reaching for the smoke alarm. After a moment, it squeaked and then went silent.

"It's okay," Emma's mom said to Zoe. "It happens to everybody. Just try to be careful." Zoe nodded, wide eyed.

Natalia reached for her glass of milk and frowned at Emma. "Caitlin likes you fine," she said. "But I can talk to her if you want."

Emma shook her head. She imagined Caitlin's

reaction if Natalia told her she had to be nicer to Emma. "Caitlin and I will work it out."

Natalia shrugged. "Well, let me know if you want me to do anything," she said, and picked up her plate and took it to the counter where the quiches were cooling.

Grandma Stephenson reached across the table and patted Emma's hand. "If this girl is Natalia's good friend, there must be *something* good about her," she said. "Maybe you should try to get to know her on her own. If Natalia likes her and Natalia likes you, there's probably something you'll like about each other."

"Maybe," Emma said doubtfully.

Zoe, listening in by the stove, shrugged. "Might be worth a try," she said. "Or you could come sit with me at lunch."

Did Zoe mind that she sat with Natalia? Emma wondered, twisting the bottom of her shirt between her hands. It hadn't seemed like she did, but it was sometimes hard to tell what Zoe felt.

"Stop trying to steal Emma," Natalia objected from the counter. She was grinning, but there was an edge to the words, like she wasn't entirely joking. Emma looked back and forth between her cousins, unsure.

Is it because of me that they're fighting? She hadn't thought of it before—was it *her* fault that her cousins didn't get along as well as they had always seemed to? *If I'm the reason they're fighting, maybe I can get them to be as close as they used to be.* Emma took a deep breath. She could do it. She would make the three of them like their cousin vow again—*not just cousins and sisters, but best friends.*

Chapter Eight

"These are going to be really cute," Emma said Saturday morning, carefully running her paintbrush around the edge of a chair seat, leaving a stripe of sunny yellow. It was just her and her mom today—Zoe was at her art class, and Natalia was babysitting. It was nice to spend some time alone with her mom for a change. The worry she'd felt around the twins lately—that they weren't as close as they used to be, and that *she* might be the reason—had become a low thrum of anxiety whenever she was with them, and it was good to be free of that worry for a while.

"I think they'll be fun." Her mom had turned one of the small round tables upside down and was painting its legs pale blue.

They had all decided to replace the long formal table in the dining room of Seaview House with several small tables and chairs, all painted in pastel candy colors. Emma and her mom had been painting for a while now this morning, and there were two other chairs, pink and light green, drying on top of newspapers on the grassy lawn beside them.

"People who come to B and Bs don't want to have to eat with a bunch of strangers," her mom had said. "This way each set of guests can have their own private table."

The sun was warm on Emma's shoulders—it didn't cool off in Maryland until much later than it did back in Seattle, and September here was just as hot as August—but it felt good. She could smell the flowers in the garden, and there were blue jays screeching raucously overhead.

"These are nice," she said to her mom. She began to paint the back of the chair with short, careful strokes.

"They are," her mom agreed. She put down her paintbrush and rolled back her shoulders, stretching. "Imagine what it'll be like when we open."

Emma could picture the bright little tables full of happy people—tourists and couples in love and families—enjoying French toast and arepas and her dad's special fruit crepes. The dining room used to be too dark, Emma thought, with heavy drapes and the long dark table. But once it was full of guests and light it would be fun. "We should get some little lacy table-cloths and replace the curtains with something that lets more light through," she suggested.

Her mom nodded. "That room's always been a little gloomy."

"We could put fresh flowers on the tables," Emma suggested. "I could cut flowers out of the garden in the summer."

"And in the winter we could make dried flower arrangements," her mom suggested. "Or do something seasonal with holly or tiny Christmas trees. Or shells and pebbles from the beach, to make people think of summer."

"That would be so cute," Emma said. "You know who will have some good ideas for things like that? Zoe."

"And Alison will, too," her mom added. "She's always been good at making places seem welcoming."

Emma thought of the big, noisy kitchen at Aunt Alison and Uncle Luis's house, and how things were a little hectic there, with so many people running in and out, but always cheerful. "Yeah," she agreed. "Their house feels really friendly."

Her mom got up and came over to crouch down by where Emma was painting. "Are you having a good time there?" she asked softly, resting her hand on Emma's back. "I haven't gotten to spend enough time with you lately. I miss you."

Emma's eyes stung. "I miss you, too," she said. "I am having a good time at Zoe and Natalia's. Mostly." She thought for a moment of telling her mom all about the tension between Natalia and Zoe, but there was something proud and determined in her that made her stop—she wanted to figure this out with them, rather than asking her mom for help.

Her mom grinned and tangled her fingers in Emma's hair. "I guess mostly is the best we can hope for," she said. "What about this friend of Natalia's whom you don't like? Do you need to talk about that?"

"No," Emma said. "I can handle it." It would be nice to get along with Caitlin, but Caitlin didn't really matter to her, not the way Zoe and Natalia did. "It's weird, though, because Zoe and Natalia don't hang out at school much. And Natalia wants me to sit with her and eat lunch with her and stuff. So I end up not spending a lot of time with Zoe at school."

Her mom frowned. "Are Natalia and Zoe fighting a lot?"

"No," Emma said slowly. "They just say they have different friends. But it's not the way I pictured that going to school with them would be."

Emma's mom gave a little laugh and pulled her fingers out of Emma's hair, smoothing it down. "Even people who love each other don't want to spend all their time together," she said. "Sometimes some space is good. Alison and I were always friends as well as twins, and we had different friends at school, too. And if you want to be with Zoe more, go sit with Zoe. Natalia doesn't own you."

Emma made a face but didn't say anything. Natalia was always saying "Sit here with me" or pulling Emma down the hall beside her. It would feel weird to get up and leave her to go with Zoe.

"If there's one thing I learned growing up as a twin," her mother said, leaning back, "it's that even when you love somebody, sometimes you just need to get away from them for a while. I know you worry, but sometimes you have to trust that people will work their own problems out."

Emma looked at her paintbrush instead of her mom, carefully focusing on covering the round sides of a carved apple with yellow paint. "Is that true even of you and Dad? Do you have to get away from him sometimes?"

Her mom flopped back in the grass and stared up at the sky. "Honestly, Emma, at this point it's the opposite. It's been so long since I've seen your dad, I just really miss him."

"I do, too," Emma said. She and her dad had a regular Sunday morning call before the brunch rush, but it wasn't the same as seeing him every day. *I hope it's not too long until we can all be together again.*

❧

Painting was much harder work than Emma had expected it to be. Her shoulders ached and the smell of the paint gave her a headache after a while. Leaving her mom still painting, Emma went upstairs to call Amelia back in Seattle.

"This house is *crazy,*" Amelia said, as Emma gave her a tour, holding up her phone to show Amelia the old ballroom that they were going to use as an event space, the big kitchen where the professional stove had just been installed, and the secret staircase.

"Look," Emma said, opening a little waist-high door in the kitchen and pointing the phone toward it. "It's a dumbwaiter. It's like a little elevator for food; you put it in and send it upstairs."

"Are you guys going to use it to give the guests break-fast in bed?" Amelia asked. "Because that would be really luxurious. You could just lie there and open a door and, *poof,* pancakes."

"I'm not sure it works anymore," Emma said. There was a rope to pull near the top of the dumbwaiter, and when Emma hesitantly touched it, it squealed alarmingly.

"Yikes," Emma said, yanking her hand back as Amelia laughed. "Sounds like a ghost lives in there!"

As Amelia told Emma about her sixth-grade home-room teacher and the new soccer team lineup—another girl on the team had taken Emma's starting spot, and they'd won their first game—Emma felt as if the place she'd left in Seattle had already been filled before she'd even found her place in Waverly. It had only been a few weeks, but everything had changed.

"I miss you," she told Amelia, feeling an ache in her chest.

There wasn't a whole lot more to say. Already, Seattle seemed really far away—well, it *was* far away—and it was almost like Emma didn't belong there anymore.

⁓◌⁓

After she hung up, Emma heard the front door opening. She peeked out of the kitchen and saw Zoe and Natalia walking in.

"Hey!" she said, surprised. "I thought you guys were busy." She glanced from one to the other, trying to figure out if they were getting along today. They seemed okay: Zoe was smiling and Natalia looked exhausted, her shoulders slumped, but not angry.

"We're both done, and we thought we'd see what you were up to," Zoe said.

Emma's mom came in from outside, too, her jeans smeared with yellow paint. "Hello, girls," she said, then took a closer look at Natalia. "Natalia, are you all right?"

Natalia moaned dramatically, casting her eyes up to the ceiling. "Never again," she said. "I am never babysitting again. At least with my own brothers, I can threaten to lock them in their rooms. Those Miller girls are *demons.*"

Emma snickered. "What did they do?"

"What didn't they do?" Natalia said, staring at Emma with large tragic brown eyes. "They had an *orange juice* fight in the kitchen. Do you know how sticky and horrible orange juice is when it's all over everything? And then one of them locked the other one in the guest bedroom. It took me twenty-five minutes to get her out."

"Their mother likes Natalia to babysit them because they're twins," Zoe said, smirking. "She thinks Natalia understands them."

"I do understand them," Natalia said, glumly. "Remember when we used to switch places all the time to fool people? They do that."

Emma's mom laughed. "I remember that. You drove your mother crazy."

"Didn't you ever do it?" Zoe asked.

Emma's mom smiled, remembering. "One year in high school, I took biology twice a day because Alison didn't like it," she said, "and Alison took English twice so I wouldn't have to read *The Scarlet Letter*, which sounded incredibly boring."

"*Mom*," Emma said, shocked.

Emma's mom blushed. "But you should never do that,"

she said quickly to Natalia and Zoe. "I'm sure I missed a lot. I should probably read *The Scarlet Letter* now to make up for it. Alison liked it."

"We couldn't get away with it anyway," Natalia said sadly. "Not now that we have different haircuts."

Zoe tucked her short hair behind her ears. "I like looking different."

Natalia frowned. "Looking the same is the *point* of being twins."

Emma felt her shoulders tense. Why did they have to needle each other like this? Eager to head off a fight, Emma asked her mom, "Can we look in the attic? Maybe we can find some stuff for my room?"

Upstairs, Zoe stared at the Christmas ornaments and fishing tackle, then behind them at the heaps of boxes and trunks and dusty furniture stretching as far as the girls could see. She looked down at her clean white shirt and pale green shorts. "This is going to be filthy," she said disapprovingly.

"You're such a princess," Natalia said, and Zoe shrugged.

"Come on, it'll be fun," Emma told them. "Don't you want to see what's back here?" Wiggling her way past a dusty fish tank and a pile of beach toys, Emma made her way to the part of the attic that was crowded with the older things, stuff that her family had been storing here for years and years.

There was a pile of books and papers in one box, and she pulled it over near a dirty window to rummage through. Not much: old Christmas cards and yellowed paperbacks that gave off that weird mildewy old book smell.

Natalia crouched next to her and dug through the box, pulling out a bunch of sewing patterns of ridiculous wide-legged seventies outfits. "Look at these," she said, and giggled. "Check out the plaid pantsuit. Who thought that was a good look?"

There was a sketchbook buried halfway down the box, and Emma pulled it out and flipped through it. There was no name on it, or on any of the drawings. The sketches were interesting: There were some detailed pictures of leaves or flowers in pencil, faded so that the pencil lines they were drawn in were hard to make out in places. On other pages there were more detailed scenes sketched out, brushed here and there with paint. One of these was of the bay, and Emma realized that it was the bay the way she saw it from the upstairs windows of this house. The water was touched with blue—watercolor, she thought—and white boats sailed across, clearly scudding under a brisk wind. They reminded her of riding in Uncle Dean's boat.

"Hey, Zoe," she called across the attic to where Zoe was trying to look at furniture without getting her clothes dirty. "Come look at these."

It took Zoe a while to pick her way to Emma, but when she looked at the sketchbook, she was absorbed. "These are really nice," she said, turning the pages carefully. Stopping on a pencil sketch of a shell, she traced her finger over it. "I didn't know anyone in the family before me drew, or painted."

Beside her, Natalia looked up from the sewing patterns. "The way the lines go on that one," Natalia said, pointing. "It's like that drawing you did on the beach last year."

They set the sketchbook carefully aside to take back with them—maybe Grandma Stephenson would be able to tell them who the artist had been.

In another box, Zoe found a program made of thick paper and bound with a ribbon. On the front was printed:

Put Your Head on My Shoulder, Waverly High School Junior-Senior Prom, 1963. "This must be from Grandma Stephenson's prom," she said, carefully lifting a dried corsage out of the box—white roses and green ribbon— that crumbled in her hand.

Emma realized that she hadn't seen her cousins like this—absorbed in the same thing—much lately. Why couldn't they always be like this?

Under the prom program was a small square suitcase, or some kind of box with a handle, Emma pulled the little suitcase out and wiped the dust off the top with the bottom of her T-shirt before she flipped the latch and opened it.

Records. The small kind that had only one song on each side. Emma pulled a few out. The Diamonds. The Platters. The Shirelles. A name she knew: Elvis Presley. These were probably Grandma's, too, from high school. It was funny to imagine her as a teenager, maybe with a high bouffant and wearing her prom dress with white gloves, like Emma had seen in pictures of dances back then.

"We've got to take these to your new room, too," Natalia said.

They lugged the records into Emma's new room. There was still no furniture, but there were paper towels, and Emma grabbed some to wipe off the suitcase and sketchbook. As she worked, she could hear her mom's voice down in the yard below the open window, with the pauses and rhythms of speech that made it clear she was on the phone. The dust came off in long gray streaks, showing that the suitcase underneath was shiny white and gold. It was satisfying to get it clean, and Emma rubbed harder.

"No, I don't understand!" Her mom's voice rose, and Emma paused, listening. She sounded really upset. Emma looked out the window.

Her mom was pacing across the lawn a couple of stories below, almost yelling into the phone. "You keep saying you want to come out here, but I don't see you doing anything about it," she said. "If you want to stay in Seattle, you should just say so instead of stringing me and Emma along."

Emma winced. Her mom was talking to her dad, *shouting* at him. Did her dad really not want to come to Waverly?

Natalia was next to her suddenly and reached to close the window. "Don't listen," she said. "Parents fight sometimes."

Emma shook her head. "Not like this." Her heart was pounding hard.

Zoe wrapped an arm around her. "I'm sure they'll work it out," she said. "It's like me and Natalia—we fight but we always make up. Right, Natalia?" Zoe turned to her sister.

Natalia grinned. "Only if you're willing to beg for my forgiveness."

Zoe rolled her eyes, and Emma felt a little better. She hoped they were right.

Chapter Nine

On the way back to Zoe and Natalia's house, Emma's mom acted totally normal. As she fiddled with the radio, driving one-handed, Emma watched her out of the corner of her eye. She didn't look angry or upset, the way she had sounded when Emma overheard her on the phone.

Should I ask her about Dad?

What if he really is going to stay in Seattle?

Emma clutched the old sketchbook in her lap tightly. Her hands were sweating, and her throat was dry with anxiety. "So, did you talk to Dad?" she asked, sounding, at least to herself, too abrupt to be casual. "I saw you on the phone."

"Oh, sure," Her mom looked straight ahead at the road, but her voice was casual. "They're still looking for a new chef to replace your father."

Maybe I'm just being dramatic. Her mom sounded so

normal. Emma didn't know what to think. She rested her forehead against the window and stared out at the passing scenery, feeling sick with tension.

From the backseat, Zoe reached up and rested her hand on Emma's shoulder, a warm comfort.

⁘ ᘇᓂ

When they got back to the house, Natalia lugged in the little suitcase of records and flipped it open. "We've got to ask Grandma about these," she said. She pulled out some of the singles in their little paper envelopes, shuffling through them. "Listen to these titles," she said, snorting with laughter, "'Mickey's Monkey'? 'Sugar Shack'? 'Mashed Potato Time'?"

"'Mashed Potato Time'?" Emma asked, laughing despite her lingering worries. "Sounds delicious."

Grandma Stephenson came in from her bedroom, leaning on her cane. She was limping, Emma noticed, but smiling, too.

"The Mashed Potato was a dance," Grandma told them. "We still had dances with steps then."

"Like the Twist?" Natalia asked. "I can do that." She twisted her hips and bent her knees, going down to the floor and coming up again.

"Very good," Grandma said. "Now go get the record player out of my room, and we'll play some of these records."

While Natalia was getting the record player, Emma and Zoe showed Grandma the sketchbook.

"This was my cousin Carolyn's," Grandma told them, turning pages. "She was interested in botany. And art, of course. We had a lot of fun together growing up. Maybe that's where Zoe gets her love of drawing."

"Cousin Carolyn?" Emma's mom asked. "I remember her from those big Christmas parties. Is she still in Colorado?"

Grandma Stephenson nodded. "She'll be tickled to hear the girls found this. Oh, look." She stopped at a pencil drawing of a teenage girl with short curly hair. The girl had freckles and big eyes and her mouth was drawn up in a mischievous smile, as if she had a secret.

"She looks kind of like you," Zoe said to Emma. "But her expression is more like Natalia's."

"That's you, isn't it, Mom?" Emma's mom asked Grandma Stephenson.

Grandma? Now that her mom had said that, Emma saw the high cheekbones and the decided sweep of her nose. It was hard to imagine Grandma so young and freckled, though. But when Emma looked at her, she saw that same smile.

"Carolyn and I had a lot of fun," Grandma repeated, shaking her head reminiscently. "Oh, good," she added as Natalia staggered in with the record player. "Put that on the table and plug it in."

"You know what weighs less than a record player?" Natalia asked, putting down the record player and shaking out her arms. "My cell phone."

"These are cool, though," Zoe said, squinting at the records.

Grandma put one of the records onto the record player and used her cane to pull herself to her feet. "For the Mashed Potato," she said, "you put your heels together"—she moved her feet into something like first position for ballet—"then you push them out." She moved so her toes were pointing at each other. "You do that a couple of times, then you kick your feet up while you do it." She demonstrated again. Emma's mom and Natalia hopped to their feet to imitate her, and Emma and Zoe followed.

Grandma put the record player's needle on the record

and, after a minute of hissing, the music began, a girl's voice singing, "It's the latest, it's the greatest . . ."

They all danced. Grandma had her hands held out at her sides and leaned on her cane as she kicked one foot up, then the other, swiveling on the balls of her feet the whole time. Emma's mom twirled around, then grabbed hold of Emma's hands and spun her. Zoe and Natalia were face-to-face, mirroring each other's movements as they swiveled.

This is nice, Emma thought, looking at them. *If I could just get them to remember how much fun they have together, maybe we could all be friends at school, too.*

The door opened and Mateo and Tomás ran in, followed by Abuelita and Aunt Alison carrying grocery bags.

"Wow, dance party!" Tomás shouted, and Mateo squealed with excitement, but Abuelita's face crumpled when she saw Grandma dancing.

"Be careful!" she said worriedly. "What if you fall?"

The song ended and the record hissed into silence. Grandma stilled and straightened.

"I'm not an invalid, Rosa," she said coolly. "I may have trouble on stairs now, but I'm hardly frail."

Abuelita stared back at her, her mouth set. "You need rest," she said. "As a registered nurse, I feel responsible for making sure you get it."

The grandmothers glared at each other, and Emma exchanged anxious looks with Zoe and Natalia. The tension in the room made Emma uncomfortable. *Can't Mom calm them down?* she wondered, but her mom was looking back and forth between them, as wary as Emma herself.

Aunt Alison plopped her grocery bags on the table. "Mom, maybe you should sit down. No one wants you to fall again."

Grandma Stephenson sighed and sat down, leaning on her cane. "Fine," she said flatly.

Later, in the twins' room, Natalia said, "I don't think it's fair the way Abuelita picks on Grandma."

Zoe shrugged, focusing on painting Emma's nails in smooth, even strokes of glittery pink. "She's not *picking* on her. She just worries that she's going to get hurt again."

Natalia leaned back against the wall and blew on her own wet nails. "She's just making Grandma mad.

Grandma's like me: If you keep telling her not to do something, she'll do it more. Plus, Grandma's a grown-up and she should be able to decide what she can do."

"Hmm. I don't want Grandma to get hurt again." Zoe finished Emma's pinky and capped the bottle. "Don't touch anything," she told her.

"Emma agrees with me, don't you, Emma?" Natalia said. "Abuelita's just being overprotective."

"I don't know." Emma rested her chin on her knees. Her chest felt hollow and achy. "I'm just tired of everybody fighting."

Zoe frowned and put the bottle of nail polish down on the bedside table. "What do you mean everybody? Who else is fighting?"

Emma felt her lips trembling. "My parents."

Zoe scooched closer and wrapped her arm around Emma's shoulders.

Natalia sighed. "I told you, don't worry about it. It doesn't mean anything that they fought."

"I don't know if my dad's coming after all," Emma whispered. It hurt just to say the words.

Natalia patted her on the leg. "I really do think you're overreacting."

Zoe glared at her sister. "Oh, *that's* helpful."

Natalia shrugged and tossed her hair back over her shoulders. "What? She is. Emma, you should just try to forget about it. If you concentrate on something else, it'll all blow over."

"Yeah, I guess," Emma said, hunching her shoulders. She wished the twins would stop fighting, too, but she didn't want to say it.

Zoe leaned forward to see Emma's face. "Do you want to talk about it some more?"

Emma shook her head. What good would it do? Natalia was probably right, anyway. If Emma just tried not to worry about it, it would go away. She was probably overreacting.

"I'm going to get ready for bed," she said, reaching for her pajamas. She tried to smile. She would think about her room at Seaview House the whole time she was brushing her teeth, she decided. If she thought really hard about where she would hang the sketch of the bay Cousin Carolyn had made and about which bed would feel right in her new, high, slanted little room, she wouldn't have space in her thoughts to worry about anything else.

Chapter Ten

Monday, Emma felt a little off all morning, itchy and restless. She doodled and stared out the window through social studies, science, and Spanish class, and ate her lunch quietly at one end of Natalia's table, listening with only half an ear to the cafeteria conversations. She kept glancing over to Zoe's table, too, wishing she could have both her cousins together the way they had been that weekend—exploring stuff in the attic, dancing with Grandma, painting each other's nails, hanging out.

Now it was gym, and Emma was grateful. When she played sports—any sports—she could narrow her focus, forget all her worries and anxious thoughts, and just *be*. Every bit of her concentrated on hitting the ball, or plunging through the water, or racing around a track. Today, they were playing soccer, one of Emma's favorite games. Soccer moved fast, there wasn't a lot of time spent just standing around on the field.

Emma sprinted after Vivian, enjoying the stretch of her own muscles as she caught up. Vivian was weaving down the field, dribbling the ball in front of her.

"I'm open!" Caitlin shouted just as Emma caught up to Vivian. Vivian tried to pass Caitlin the ball, but Emma intercepted it and kicked it far down the field. She passed it to Natalia, who made the goal.

The whistle blew, and Emma leaned forward onto her knees, catching her breath.

"Good hustle out there." Mrs. Brandon, the gym teacher, patted her on the back, and Emma smiled at her, pleased.

"Nice, Emma!" Natalia cheered, running over to give her a high five. "Good game, you guys," she told Vivian and Caitlin. Vivian grinned back at her, but Caitlin just nodded, her lips tight. *Sore loser*, Emma thought. She wasn't surprised. Caitlin acted like the kind of girl who expected to always get her way.

But after Natalia had run off to talk to another friend and the other kids around them had also wandered away, Caitlin suddenly leaned in toward Emma. "Show-off," she hissed, her face scrunched up.

"What?" Emma flinched backward, startled by the venom in Caitlin's voice.

"You think you're *so* great," Caitlin said. "You don't belong here." She whipped around and marched away.

Emma watched her go, feeling a little shaken. *You don't belong here* was meant to hurt, and it did—but Emma knew she had as much right as anyone else to be here.

Caitlin had clearly waited until Natalia and Vivian were out of earshot before she said anything nasty to Emma. Biting her lip, Emma saw Caitlin walk up to Natalia farther down the field, smiling like nothing was wrong.

Emma hadn't liked the way Natalia brushed it off when Emma and Zoe had told her that Caitlin didn't like Emma. Now it was clearer than ever that Caitlin had a problem with her. But how could Emma make Natalia see Caitlin's meanness without causing even more trouble?

"Everybody in!" Mrs. Brandon shouted, blowing her whistle again, and Emma followed the rest of the class back into the building. Emma noticed that Caitlin walked next to Natalia, focused on her, talking eagerly.

"Hey," Zoe said in the locker room, nudging her as they pulled their clothes out of their lockers. "You okay? You seem spaced out."

"I'm just thinking," Emma said.

She could *tell* Natalia what Caitlin had said to her today. Natalia might not want to believe her friend was being mean to Emma when all Emma had to report were some mean looks, but maybe Natalia would listen if Emma told her what Caitlin had just said.

"Thinking so hard you're going to be late for class," Zoe commented, and Emma realized her cousin had changed back into her regular school clothes while Emma was still in her gym uniform. Emma hurriedly began to pull off her gym shirt.

"Go ahead," she said. "I'll catch up."

If one of her friends was being mean to Natalia or Zoe, Emma thought, she would want to know. And if Natalia learned the truth, she would take Emma's side, Emma felt certain—Natalia was fiercely loyal. Zoe would back her up, too.

But . . .

Caitlin was one of Natalia's best friends. Emma didn't want to be the reason they had a falling-out—even if it wasn't really her fault. There had to be a better way. Climbing into her clothes, Emma made up her mind. She wasn't going to go to her cousins. She lived here now, she *belonged* here, no matter what Caitlin said. But she didn't want to force Natalia to choose between her and Caitlin, even if she knew Natalia would choose her cousin over her friend.

No, Emma decided. She wouldn't say anything. Somehow, she would find a way to fix this herself.

But she knew it wasn't going to be easy.

In English class, Mr. Thomas wrote on the board in big letters: BIRDY PROJECT.

"We're pretending to be little birdies?" a boy named Noah asked, and made weird squawking noises, flapping his arms.

"Settle down," Mr. Thomas said. "Instead of a paper, you're going to do a project about *Catherine, Called Birdy* in groups of four." He paused while a buzz of whispers broke out: people leaning toward each other and picking partners.

"What kind of project?" Bridget asked, her hand in the air.

"Well, that's up to you," Mr. Thomas told them. "You could make a scrapbook about medieval life, or write a journal like Birdy's in the book, showing her world in four different seasons. You could make a short illuminated manuscript, or act out a scene from the book. Mostly, I want to see something that you think is interesting or have enjoyed."

"Are you assigning partners?" Noah asked.

"I'll let you pick," Mr. Thomas replied.

Emma looked around nervously. Zoe was whispering to Louise, as Aaron at the back of the room threw a ball of paper to get the attention of his friend Max.

"Settle down!" Mr. Thomas called again. "We're going to do this in an orderly fashion." He pointed at Madison, who sat in the front seat of the first row, a few seats down from Emma. "Madison, choose three partners."

"Um," Madison said, looking startled. "Kayla and, uh, Tamara. And Isabel."

"Good." He pointed at Noah, then at Hannah, and they each chose partners. Emma was next. Mr. Thomas pointed at her. "Emma, choose your partners."

Emma looked toward Natalia and caught Caitlin's eye. Caitlin was frowning, her lower lip pushing out sulkily.

Emma hesitated. She wanted to work with Natalia and Zoe both. Although would they want to work together? She didn't quite understand what was going on with them at school. But maybe this was the opportunity she'd wanted to get them together. The three of them could be the tight little team she'd imagined.

But who else? Vivian was fun. Or one of Zoe's friends. But . . .

Suddenly, Emma had an idea about how she might fix the Caitlin problem without blowing up the friendship between Caitlin and Natalia.

"Emma, are you with us?" Mr. Thomas asked.

"Zoe, Natalia, and—Caitlin," she said, feeling her cheeks heat up. It was *possible* that this was a terrible idea.

Natalia gave a muted cheer. Caitlin's eyes widened and her jaw dropped.

Even if this ended up being a bad idea in the end, Emma couldn't help thinking Caitlin's baffled expression was pretty funny. But then Caitlin snapped her mouth shut, and her eyes narrowed with suspicion, still staring at Emma.

Emma dropped her own eyes to the top of her desk, suddenly feeling uncomfortable. She realized there was a pretty high possibility it was just going to be awful. Fixing anything would require Caitlin to cooperate at least a little bit.

Emma swallowed hard. What had Grandma Stephenson said? *If this girl is Natalia's good friend, there must be something good about her.* Emma wasn't going to go through school fighting with her cousin's good friend—that sounded exhausting and would be terrible for Natalia, who would be caught in the middle. Emma was going to have to find the good thing about Caitlin.

❧

Caitlin hurried down the hall toward the school library a little ahead of Emma, Zoe, and Natalia. Even Caitlin's back looked annoyed, Emma thought.

Mr. Thomas had sent them to the library to work— *quietly,* he said. "No talking in the halls," he reminded them sharply now, hushing a rising buzz of conversation.

I don't need to worry about that, Emma thought glumly. *One of my partners doesn't* want *to talk to me.* She was feeling more and more sure that this had been a mistake. *Maybe I'm going to lose Zoe and Natalia if we can't get along,* she thought, twisting her hands nervously together. *I've dragged them into a problem I don't know how to fix.*

Even Natalia was picking up on Caitlin's anger now. She was unusually silent, glancing uneasily between them. Zoe was looking through the book as she walked, ignoring the tension between the others.

They settled at one of the small tables in the library. Caitlin huffed impatiently as she opened her notebook and got out a pen. Emma caught Zoe looking at her quizzically.

Emma's mouth felt dry, and she had to swallow several times before she could talk. "So," she said at last. "What do you think we should do?"

"Maybe a scrapbook?" Natalia said. "We could get pictures of medieval things, and . . ." She covered her eyes and dropped her head onto the table. "I haven't actually read the book yet," she muttered.

"Natalia!" Zoe glared at her exasperatedly.

Natalia sat up, half laughing. "Well, all the school clubs are starting up again, and you *know* I would rather do a thousand math problems than a reading assignment . . ."

"You always do stuff like this," Zoe said, annoyed.

Emma tightened her fingers on her pen until they hurt. Maybe this *had* been a mistake. If she was just going to give the twins more reasons to fight at school, it might have been better to leave them apart.

"It's fine," she said quickly, before Natalia could snap back at Zoe. "It's a good book, and we'll come up with something really good to do."

Caitlin sighed. "I'm sure you have some great idea, Emma," she said flatly. "After all, you already know all about it."

"I just read it before," Emma said, feeling defensive. "It's not a big deal."

"Whatever," Caitlin said under her breath.

Emma had been planning to be nice to Caitlin, but that kind of depended on Caitlin not being a total jerk. "Look," she said quietly. "Do you have some kind of problem with me?"

"I'm sure she doesn't have a problem with you," Natalia said. Her brown eyes were huge and worried. "You guys just . . . rub each other the wrong way."

Zoe snorted and started looking through her book again.

"I don't have a problem with you," Caitlin said. She turned a page over in her notebook, then twisted her pen between her fingers, capping and uncapping it. Finally, she burst out, "I just think you're a show-off, that's all."

"No, she's not!" Natalia objected, but Caitlin was staring at Emma, her face hard.

"The very first day, you started telling everyone how you already knew everything in this book," Caitlin said. "And you're always pushing ahead and showing off in gym class. And trying to get Natalia's attention and everybody else's, too."

"That's not true!" Emma insisted. She knew she wasn't a show-off—if anything, she'd felt lost and at the edges of things since they moved here. It was true that Natalia had been paying attention to her, but Natalia was her cousin, and she was helping Emma find her place in school; Emma couldn't be blamed for that, could she? And the other things Caitlin had mentioned—sports, and the coincidence of having read the book—were just who Emma was. Was she supposed to lie about books and hold herself back from winning games?

"Cate, you're not being fair," Natalia said unhappily. "You've totally got the wrong idea about Emma!"

"Emma's good at sports," Zoe said, looking up from her book to glare at Caitlin. "She's not pushing ahead, she's just playing better than you."

Caitlin made a sour face, as if she had just bitten into a lemon.

The bell rang, putting an abrupt end to the conversation.

"Well, I guess we'll figure out what we want to do tomorrow," Natalia said, forcing a bright tone.

Caitlin's just jealous. Emma was sure of it, but she bit back her words. If she wanted to get along with Caitlin— which she did, if only for Natalia's sake —then she needed to make her *less* jealous—somehow.

Chapter Eleven

"Caitlin's just used to having most of Natalia's attention," Zoe told Emma as they walked home from the bus that day, Tomás running ahead of them. Natalia had stayed late for service club, so they had been able to discuss everything that had happened with Caitlin. "She and Natalia have been besties for a long time. She'll get used to you and stop acting so weird."

"It would be easier if *you* were Natalia's best friend," Emma said.

Tomás slammed the house door open in front of them and ran in, shouting, "Mommy!" but Zoe paused on the porch and looked thoughtfully at Emma, her eyes warm.

"Listen," she said. "Natalia and I are definitely friends, even at school. We hang out with different people because we like to do different things. And because she likes a whole crowd of people around her and I want just a couple of friends I'm really close to. But we're always *really* best friends, no matter who we're with." She paused and half smiled, a dimple popping up in one cheek. "Better than best friends. *Family.*"

She squeezed Emma's arm, and Emma got what Zoe was saying, warmth spreading through her. Emma was that, too—better than a friend. She was like Zoe's and Natalia's sister—and they were like sisters to her.

"Okay," she said. "Okay, I get it." She followed Zoe into the house.

"Girls!" Aunt Alison said. She, Emma's mom, Grandma Stephenson, and Abuelita were waiting for them. Tomás and Mateo were wolfing down cookies and fruit. "We're taking your grandmothers over to look at where we are with Seaview House. Drop your bags and let's go!"

"Can't we have a snack first?" Emma pleaded. She wanted Grandma and Abuelita to see the improvements that had been made since the last time they were there, but she was also practically starving. Lunch had been a long time ago.

"I've got you covered. Cookies and string cheese," her mom said, handing her and Zoe each a paper bag. "The boys are already eating theirs!" She grinned at Tomás and Mateo. "You can eat yours in the car. And there just might be something to snack on at the inn, too."

They took Aunt Alison's minivan instead of walking because of Grandma Stephenson's hip. As they pulled up the drive to the house, Grandma exclaimed with pleasure, "Oh, now that looks lovely!" The long porch that wrapped around the house had been freshly repainted, and hanging baskets of red geraniums hung at intervals from its ceiling. Blue-painted chairs—some rockers, some armchairs—sat in a row on the porch. Emma could imagine them filled with happy, chattering guests.

Inside, Grandma paused and looked around. Trying to see it through her eyes, Emma realized how much had changed. The last time Grandma Stephenson had been here, most of the downstairs had been under construction.

Now, the wooden floors were polished and shining. The rooms had been repainted, the living room in a soft gold, the halls white, and the dining room in a light blue. They weren't fully furnished yet, but there were chairs and tables here and there, and you could get the idea of where things would be.

"Awesome!" Tomás shouted. He kicked off his shoes, then ran and slid across the wide empty floorboards of the living room.

"Me, too! Tomás, wait!" Mateo followed him.

"The new bedrooms won't be finished for a while," Aunt Alison said. She looked nervous, her gaze flicking back and forth from Grandma Stephenson to the newly changed rooms. "But we thought that if we get the public rooms up and running first, we'll be able to start hosting events—weddings and parties and that sort of thing—while we're finishing the guest rooms."

"We're going to move the piano in here," Emma's mom said, gesturing at a corner of the living room. "It'll be nice to have some music when the guests are mingling." Her voice was high and quick, as if she, too, was nervous. Both moms were watching Grandma eagerly for a reaction.

"Well, I think it looks lovely," Abuelita said warmly. "I never realized what a gorgeous view of the bay you got from these windows, Julia. Getting rid of those heavy drapes lets us see it."

Grandma nodded slowly. "It certainly is brighter in here now," she said.

"I think it looks great," Zoe added loyally. "And it still feels like Seaview House, even though it's different. It's like the face of the house is the same, but it's wearing different makeup."

Leaning on her cane, Grandma walked into the dining room. "Oh," she said, sounding surprised. "All these little tables."

"Mom and I painted those ourselves," Emma told her. "We liked all the pretty colors. Aren't they cute?" But Emma saw that Grandma Stephenson's eyes looked a little red around the corners, as if she might be holding back tears. "Is it okay?" she asked. "I know it's different than before . . ." Emma trailed off. Her mom and Aunt Alison had worked so hard. And it *did* look good, Emma thought. But different—definitely different. She bit her lip. It would be terrible if Grandma hated what they'd done to Seaview House.

Grandma brushed a hand across her eyes and gave a little laugh. "Of course I like it," she said shakily. "It's just a change is all."

"And change can be good, right?" Emma said, still worried. "That's what we decided, isn't it?"

Grandma's face softened, and she looked around the dining room again. "Yes," she said softly. "And these little tables are very charming."

"And what about where your family is going to live, Amy?" Grandma asked Emma's mom.

"Well, it's all the way up at the top of the house, you know," Emma's mom said, frowning. "It might be too hard a climb."

"Nonsense, I'm not too feeble to get around my own house yet," Grandma said, her chin coming forward like Natalia's did when she wasn't going to give in on something.

Instead of taking the secret staircase, they went up the front stairs because they were wider and not as steep and had big landings to rest on. Grandma Stephenson climbed with an air of determination, one hand on the banister, the other firmly on her cane, which she steadied herself on each time she climbed a step. The little boys ran on ahead, but Zoe, Emma, and their moms kept pace with Grandma's slow progress.

Abuelita fussed along behind her. "Be *careful*, Julia," she said. "It's such a long way."

"This might take me a while, but I'm not going to fall, Rosa," Grandma Stephenson said grimly. "I'm stiff, not wobbly."

Upstairs, Grandma peeked into the half-finished rooms and admired how the apartment had been built out of empty attic space. It was still mostly unfurnished, but Emma had decided on the big bed with the drawers underneath, and her mom had moved it into her room the day before.

"It looks great, Mom," Emma said, pleased. She felt like the bed gave the room a cozy feel, even though it wasn't furnished yet otherwise.

"I always liked that bed," Grandma told her. "It used to be in the spare room when I was growing up, and my mother had it put up in the attic because she hated bending down to the drawers."

"I don't mind bending down," Emma said.

"They're big drawers," Tomás said thoughtfully. "Do you think we could fit Mateo in one?"

"Please don't try," Aunt Alison said, shepherding the little boys out of Emma's room.

"It's going to be fun to have you all living in Seaview House," Grandma said, gazing around the apartment.

Downstairs again, Aunt Alison herded everyone back into the dining room just as Natalia burst in the front door.

"I saw your note when I got home from service club," she said cheerfully. "I am *starving*. Feed me."

"If you all want to sit down, Amy and I have some samples of hors d'oeuvres for you." Aunt Alison smoothed her skirt down over her hips and headed for the kitchen, followed by Emma's mom.

A few minutes later, Aunt Alison and Emma's mom reappeared, carrying several platters of little finger foods.

"We're thinking we might have a cocktail hour at the B and B," Emma's mom explained. "Give the guests a nice snack and some wine before they head out for dinner."

Emma looked at the platter her mom put down in the center of the table. "These look really good," she said, "but I thought Dad was going to do the cooking for the B and B."

"He is," her mom said without looking at her, carefully filling small plates for the little boys. "But he's not here yet. And we wanted to figure out some ideas."

"He's coming before the B and B opens, right?" Zoe asked, with a glance at Emma.

"Of course he is," Aunt Alison told her firmly. She turned to Grandma Stephenson. "Try these, Mom; they're mushroom and feta. And the mini quiches have spinach in them."

"Ew!" Tomás said, sliding out of his chair. "Come on, Mateo." Mateo made a face and followed Tomás out into the living room. After a minute, Emma could hear the swish and thump of the boys sliding across the floor.

"There's these tiny fruit tarts, too," Aunt Alison called after them. "I think you'll like these—"

"Too late, you lost them," Zoe said, reaching for a fruit tart.

Emma bit into one of the mushroom-feta things, which was encased in crisp golden pastry. "This is good," she said. "But not as good as what Dad makes." Her mother's lips tightened, and Emma wished she could take it back. "I'm sorry," she said quickly. Her chest felt tight.

Her mom's face softened. "No, it's fine. We want your honest opinions. We're going to be serving them to people who don't already love us." She patted Emma's knee. "Don't worry, you're helping."

"On the other hand, the fruit tarts are *amazing*," Zoe said, reaching for another. "I could eat, like, ten of these."

There was a pause in the conversation, a pause full of munching and lots of appreciative noises, and then Grandma Stephenson asked, "And how is school going, girls?"

Zoe shrugged. "Same old, same old," she said.

"How about you, Emma?" Aunt Alison asked.

Emma swallowed her bite of fruit tart. Zoe was right, they *were* delicious. "We three and Caitlin are all working on a *Catherine, Called Birdy* project for English class," she said.

"With Caitlin?" her mom asked, reaching for one of the cheesy things. "That's the girl who was picking on you, right? You're friends with her now?"

"Sort of," Emma said slowly. The real answer was *No, but I hope we can learn to tolerate each other*, but she didn't want to say that in front of Natalia.

"She's just jealous of Emma," Zoe said, rolling her eyes. "She'll get over it."

Natalia crossed her arms defensively. "Caitlin's a good person. We've been friends for a long time; I think she just worries that I'm not going to be as good friends with her if I'm hanging out with Emma."

"Like I said," Zoe said. "Jealous."

"That's not okay," Aunt Alison said, frowning. "I'm surprised at Caitlin. Maybe I should call her mother."

"*Please* don't," Emma groaned. "I'm handling it." She explained her plan. "She's just worried that I'm taking her place with Natalia. If we can all work together, she'll see she doesn't need to worry." *And maybe I can bring Zoe and Natalia together at school*, she thought, but didn't say.

Emma's mom looked at her dubiously. "Are you sure?"

"Emma's right," Zoe broke in. "She's doing the perfect thing. No adults needed." Emma smiled at her cousin, grateful for the support, and Zoe grinned back.

"Children need to learn to handle this kind of thing by themselves," Grandma Stephenson said. Taking hold of her cane, she began to slowly get to her feet again. "And I would like a fork for this little tart. It's very tasty, but it's going to make my hands sticky."

"I'll get it for you, Mom," Aunt Alison said, jumping to her feet, but Grandma shook her head.

"Nonsense," she said. "You may have put a fancy new stove in my kitchen, but I assume the silverware drawer is still in the same place."

"You sit right back down, Julia," Abuelita said, bouncing to her feet. "After that long climb up and down the stairs, you need to take it easy for a while. *I* will get you a fork."

"I'm perfectly fine," Grandma Stephenson said indignantly, but Abuelita was already heading for the kitchen. As the door swung shut behind her, Grandma turned to the others with such an exaggerated grimace that Emma couldn't help laughing.

"She waits on me hand and foot," Grandma hissed in a whisper. "It's driving me insane."

"She's just trying to help, Mom," Emma's mom said.

"I'm aware of that." Grandma dropped back into her seat and sighed. "She's really very kind."

"Maybe it's like me and Caitlin," Emma said thoughtfully. There was something about the way Abuelita spoke up whenever Grandma tried to do something.

"Oh, no," Emma's mom said. "Emma, Abuelita's just overprotective. She doesn't want her to get hurt again."

"I know that," Emma said. She tried to put her

thoughts into words. "But it's like . . . Abuelita was used to being the only grandmother in the house. Then, when Grandma Stephenson moved in, she wasn't so sure of her place anymore. So she makes herself more important by taking care of Grandma, even more than Grandma needs. She's not being mean at all. But it's coming a little bit from the same place as Caitlin's meanness to me."

"Interesting," Grandma said. "You know, you could be right."

"Maybe she needs something to do so she knows how important she is," Emma said. "I mean, I really do think Caitlin's going to have good ideas for our project. She has lots of experience with performing, so a class presentation like this seems right up her alley. I'm hoping that I can find a way to make her see that."

The kitchen door swung open, and Abuelita came back in. "Found one!" she said brightly. "Now you just take it easy, Julia. Can I get you one of these cheesy things? Have you tried them?"

Grandma shot Emma a smile. "Thank you," she said, half to Abuelita, half to Emma. "I think I will try it."

Chapter Twelve

Back in the library the next day, Caitlin stared at Emma coolly, twirling a pen between her fingers.

With an inward sigh, Emma smiled at her. "How are you?" she asked.

Caitlin shrugged. "Okay," she said. She didn't ask how Emma was.

"So you've done community theater, right?" Emma tried again, opening her own notebook.

"Yeah," said Caitlin, looking surprised and suspicious.

"I was thinking that maybe we could do a scene from the book," Emma said. "Since you can act, it might be the most fun thing to do."

Natalia and Zoe joined them just then, each clutching an armload of books.

"That's a great idea!" Natalia said, overhearing Emma.

"Sounds like fun," Zoe said. "I could make a backdrop to hang up that looks like a medieval house."

"I guess we could," Caitlin said coldly, still fiddling with her pen.

"I don't know a lot about theater, though," Emma said to her. "Is there a place in the book that would make a good scene?"

"I don't know," Caitlin said, still sounding unfriendly, but she was turning the pages of the book and looked more interested than she sounded. Emma waited.

"We could combine a bunch of scenes into one," Caitlin said finally. "All these suitors who are all doing things like wiping their noses on the tablecloth or being totally pompous. And she does different things to get rid of them." She finally raised her head and made eye contact with Emma again, although there was a nasty glint in her eye. "You'd have to pretend to be a lot of different horrible old men," she said.

"I don't mind," Emma said. "It sounds funny."

"What about me?" Natalia asked, interested.

"You could be her dad," Caitlin said. "He's really mean to her. You could whack me on the head and try to talk all the old men into marrying me."

Emma noticed that Caitlin had assumed *Emma* would be the one who acted out the horrible old men, while Caitlin got to play the heroine. It might be kind of embarrassing to play the suitors, but it probably *would* be funny.

And it would be worth it, Emma thought, as she and Caitlin started going through the book to find the different courting scenes, to not have an enemy anymore.

Natalia was watching Emma with shining eyes, clearly aware of how Emma was working to make friends with Caitlin, or at least to get along.

Zoe was writing down notes instead of arguing with Natalia.

Emma hoped she was making progress, but it was hard to tell.

"Okay, I know I wasn't much help yesterday," Natalia said, "but I read more of the book last night." She spread out the pile of books she and Zoe had brought with them. "Since we're acting out a scene, maybe this costume book I grabbed will be useful."

Emma stared at the book Natalia held up. *Elementary Costume Design* showed a person posed in an elaborate spider costume on the cover. "I think you're getting carried away. This is just a class project. We can't sew a bunch of different costumes in time. And how would I change clothes?"

"There's got to be something we can do," Natalia said. "Otherwise, anyone who hasn't read the whole book is going to think there's just one really persistent suitor."

"Um, I think everyone in class has read the whole book," Emma said. "Except you."

"No, you might be right," Caitlin said. She took the book from Natalia and started to flip through it. "Not about people not having read the book. But we could do really simple costumes to make the suitors look different from each other. See?" Caitlin seemed to be so interested that she forgot to sound hostile. She pushed the book forward so the others could look at it. "This shows how to make a beard out of yarn. If one of the suitors had a beard—or we could even do a couple of beards, like a gray one and a brown one—it would be clear they were different people."

"Yes!" Zoe said, pleased. "I could make beards easily."

"And if we do costumes we might get extra credit. I'm definitely going to need extra credit in English eventually," Natalia added.

"And here"—Caitlin flipped over a few pages—"this shows different ways to tie cloth. If we got a big piece of red cloth, maybe we could tie it like a cloak, or sort of like a shirt, or like some kind of scarf thing."

"Huh," said Emma, looking at the pictures. She could see how this would work. It might not look all that medieval, but it would be clear she was playing different characters. "Caitlin, these are great ideas. This could really work."

Caitlin didn't say anything, but she didn't glare at Emma, either. As she dipped her head to look back at the book, her mouth tilted into almost a smile.

At the end of the day, Zoe had already climbed on the bus, and Emma and Natalia were about to follow her when Emma heard her mother calling.

"Emma!" Her mom jogged up to them, breathing hard. "I'm glad I caught you," she said.

"Is something wrong?" Emma asked. But her mom was smiling.

"I just want to spend a little time with my girl," her mom said. "I was driving by and I thought I'd stop and pick you up and we could go out for hot chocolate or something." Her smile dimmed a little. "I never imagined it would take so long for us to be living in the same house again."

It made Emma feel a little better to realize her mom was missing Emma as much as Emma was missing her. The occasional afternoon or evening with the whole extended family just wasn't the same. And without Dad, everything just felt . . . off.

"Are Zoe and I invited, too, or just Emma?" Natalia asked.

"Just Emma if you don't mind, Natalia," Emma's mom said, and Emma was grateful. She loved her cousins, but it wouldn't be the same if they came, too. "Tell your mom that Emma's with me and she'll be back before dinner."

"Oh, sure," Natalia said amiably. "Just leave me and Zoe to bear the burden of snack time with Tomás and Mateo alone. You haven't seen true horror till you've seen my little brothers competing to see who can put the most stuff in their mouths."

"They're not *so* bad. Pretty bad, though," Emma said, and her mother laughed.

They watched together as the school bus pulled out, Natalia and Zoe both waving from different windows. Emma's mom slung an arm around her shoulders.

"I miss seeing you every day," her mom said, "but the good thing about your staying at Alison and Luis's for so long is how much time you're spending with your cousins. I've always felt a little guilty about your being an only child. Now you get to see what it's like to have brothers and sisters."

Emma thought of Tomás and Mateo's disgusting competitions—the food *definitely* wasn't the worst of it, she'd caught them arguing over who had the biggest boogers—and Natalia's snoring, and the way that Zoe always hogged the bathroom and made everyone run late for school.

"I think I'm okay with being an only child," she said. Then she thought of how funny and cute Mateo and Tomás were a lot of the time, and how much fun she and Zoe and Natalia had together, and added, "But cousins are good. I like cousins. I mean, we're almost like sisters."

At Sweet Jane's, Emma and her mom went to the far

end of the shop and sat on pink chairs on either side of a wobbly little white-topped table.

"What do you want with your hot chocolate?" her mom asked, looking over the menu.

"Hmm." Emma considered. She almost said cheesecake, which would be rich and creamy and satisfying, but then she saw, in the bakery case nearest to them, rows of crispy little sandwich cookies in all the colors of a pastel rainbow. "Ooh, definitely macarons."

"Sounds good," her mom said. "Maybe we can take some back for the other kids."

"Sure, they'll love them," Emma said. "Zoe likes hazelnut best, and Natalia likes raspberry. The boys will eat anything."

When the hot chocolate came, it was topped with a puff of whipped cream swirled with chocolate syrup, and it was delicious. Emma spooned the whipped cream off the top, letting it melt in her mouth. When she was done with the whipped cream, she alternated sips of the sweet rich hot chocolate with small bites of crispy macaron.

"Alison and I talked to a florist this morning," her mom told her. "If we start off doing events like weddings and parties before the B and B opens, we'll need connections like that. I'm thinking that, even when we're not doing events, we should have fresh flower arrangements in the entryway."

"Classy," Emma said. "Seaview House always smells like flowers in the summer anyway." She could have roses in her own slanted-ceiling attic bedroom every day during the summer, she thought, and smiled.

"You seem happy. School was better today?" her mom asked.

"Yeah," said Emma. "We got a lot done on our English project, and at lunch Caitlin actually spoke to me. By Christmas, I'm sure we'll be the best of friends."

Emma's mom laughed. "It seems like you're really settling in here," she commented.

"I guess I am," Emma said, slightly surprised. "It took a while, but I think Zoe and Natalia and I are going to have fun together at school." She thought her plan was working—Zoe and Natalia were fighting less, and they were both having fun with the *Birdy* scene.

She had felt like such an outsider at the beginning of school, and that hadn't really been very long ago. But now she was more comfortable. She'd like to meet more people, though, people who liked the same things she liked. Zoe had the right idea: You loved your family and you counted on each other, but you needed other people, too. "I think I might try out for the soccer team," she said.

"Good idea," her mom said. "We should try to find you a new swim team, too."

"I'm not sure I'll feel all the way at home until Dad's here, though," Emma said softly. She glanced up at her mother, feeling weirdly nervous. "When is he coming?" Her voice came out softer and more anxious than she'd wanted it to.

Her mom looked a little flushed. "I don't know, Emma," she said. "I'm sure it'll be soon. *Please* don't worry."

Anxiety uncurled and expanded inside Emma like some kind of growing vine, stretching all the way through her limbs. Why was this taking so long? Was this normal? It had been weeks and weeks since her dad had been supposed to come out.

Is he really coming?

She tried not to think about it, but her mouth felt dry from nervousness, and she took a deep swig of her hot chocolate. Her mom kept talking about the bed-and-breakfast, and about how this weekend they should figure out what they needed for the downstairs rooms. Her mom thought maybe they should put up some wallpaper, and Emma made noises to show that she was listening. But really, one worried thought kept circling through her mind: *Maybe we'll never all be together again.*

When the hot chocolate and macarons were all gone, her mom got to her feet. "I'm just going to run to the restroom before we go," she said, and Emma nodded.

Alone at the table, she looked at her mother's phone, sitting beside her empty plate.

It was wrong to snoop on other people's phones.

Emma did it anyway.

There was nothing much in her mom's email: messages about the contractors, receipts and shipping notices for stuff she'd ordered online, a long chatty email from a friend of her mom's back home that didn't say anything important. Glancing up to make sure her mother wasn't coming back yet, Emma closed her mom's email and opened her text messages.

She found it almost at once. A short text exchange between her mom and her dad. It felt like something that came right after a fight.

From her dad: What do you expect me to do, then?

From her mom: I just realized you're NEVER coming out, are you?

Emma stared down at the phone. She felt shocked and yet like she'd known it all along: Her dad was never coming. They were never going to be that tight little family unit—never, never, never again.

Chapter Thirteen

Emma pressed her face against her air mattress in the twins' room, hot tears running slowly down her cheeks, dripping off the sides of her nose.

"Why didn't you ask your mom about it?" Natalia asked softly, patting her on the back.

"I don't know." Emma turned to the side to look at her cousins miserably and wiped some of the tears away with the back of her hand. "I didn't want her to know I'd been snooping on her phone." Another fat tear forced its way out, and she choked on a sob. "She might not tell me the truth anyway. When I asked when he was coming, she just said she didn't know."

Zoe was sitting on the floor next to the air mattress, rolling the fringe of the rug between her fingers. "But you don't know that for sure, do you? I mean, what she wrote sounds like something someone might just say in a fight because they're frustrated."

Emma shook her head slowly, the air mattress squeaking under her. "I don't see how I could have misunderstood. It was really straightforward." She closed her eyes and another tear slipped out. Her eyes felt red and raw, and she was tired of crying.

Her cousins sat next to her, Natalia's hand on her back, Zoe staying nearby, and Emma felt a little stronger with them there. Having Zoe and Natalia comforted her. She wasn't alone.

After a while, she stopped crying and just lay there, feeling weak and washed out with tears. "I don't know what to do," she said dully.

"Nobody can think straight when they're this upset," Zoe said. "Here"—she handed Emma a box of tissues—"blow your nose, and then go wash your face with cool water."

Emma blew and, with what felt like an enormous effort, got to her feet and went into the bathroom. In the mirror, her eyes were bloodshot and her face blotchy with tears. The cool water, though, was refreshing on her hot skin.

When she got back to the twins' bedroom, they were

standing by the door waiting for her. Zoe had a couple of sketchbooks under one arm and some pencils clutched in her hand.

"Come down to the beach with us," she said. "When I'm upset, I go down there to draw, and it really helps me. It'll clear your mind."

"I'm not an artist," Emma said reluctantly, but Zoe grinned.

"Everybody's an artist," she said. "And it doesn't matter anyway. It's just for fun."

Natalia whistled for Riley, and the dog trailed behind as they crossed the road and scrambled down the hill to the beach. A breeze off the bay lifted Emma's hair and cooled her cheeks. It was late afternoon and the beach was partly sunny, partly in shadow. There was no one there but them.

"What do I do?" Emma asked, feeling awkward.

"Come on," Zoe said. They walked down to the edge of the water together, and Zoe found half a clamshell, ridged like a fan. Sitting down on the sand, Zoe laid the shell between them.

"Your clothes are going to get all sandy," Natalia warned, but Emma shrugged and sat down, too.

"Now we draw," Zoe said, handing Emma a sketchbook and a pencil. "Don't worry about whether it's good or not, just draw what you see."

Hesitantly, Emma put the tip of her pencil on the sketchpad. The shell had little corners next to the point, she saw, almost like a bow tie. She tried to draw the shape and got what she thought was a pretty good approximation. *The lines on the shell,* she thought, *they're deeper near the rounded end,* and she tried to draw that, too.

"I'll look for more stuff," Natalia said. She called to Riley and ran down the beach, too full of energy to sit and draw.

Emma and Zoe stayed where they were, and drew and drew. Sometimes Emma peeked at Zoe's paper to see how she drew something, how she made contours and shadow on her paper. Her drawing wasn't as good as Zoe's—nowhere near as good—but it didn't matter. Zoe was right, Emma thought, when she was really concentrating on her drawing, her brain and her eyes and her hand were all connected, and too full and busy to think about anything else. And Zoe was a warm, comforting presence beside her.

Natalia brought back the best of her finds, laying

them in the sand next to Emma and Zoe, and they flipped over to the next pages in their sketchbooks and drew them, too.

They didn't talk much, although when Natalia triumphantly brought over an empty turtle shell, Zoe looked up long enough to say, "She brought a dead horseshoe crab over to me once. I wouldn't draw it, though. It *smelled*."

"I was young and foolish then," Natalia said. "I wouldn't touch one now. But I still think it would have been cool to draw."

Gradually, Emma felt her mind clearing. Even the motion of drawing—the pencil's strokes on the paper—was soothing. And, even though she was worried about her father, it was satisfying to see Zoe and Natalia working together.

A gull screeched overhead, and then another, louder screech came from more nearby. A screech that, somehow, didn't sound quite right. Emma looked up to see Natalia poised on top of a heap of sand, the remains of someone's sand castle. Natalia stared at her and screeched like a gull again, poking her head forward like one of the birds. She flapped her arms and hopped a little, and Emma, to her own surprise, choked back a laugh. *An hour ago, I felt like I would never laugh again.* "Weirdo," she said affectionately.

Pleased with herself, Natalia hopped off the sand castle and sat down next to them. Riley came and flopped down in the sand, panting loudly.

The shadows were getting longer. *It must be getting close to dinnertime.* Emma closed her sketchbook.

"I'm okay now," she said. She looked at Zoe. "Thank you," she said, and Zoe nodded. "But now I have to figure out what to do. I can't—I can't pretend I never read those messages and just wait to see what happens."

"No." Natalia wrapped her arms around her legs, thinking. "I know," she said. "We can go undercover and find out your dad's plans!"

"What are you talking about?" Emma asked skeptically.

"We could call Harvest Moon pretending to be restaurant reviewers or something," Natalia suggested. "And we could ask about if they're getting a new chef. That way, we'd know if your dad's planning to stay there or not."

It might work, Emma supposed. Whatever they said at the restaurant, it would be a clue to her parents' plans.

Zoe, though, cocked an eyebrow. "I'm not sure that's such a great idea," she said slowly.

"Yeah, maybe not," Natalia agreed. "It's a little too wacky sitcom."

Looking at Emma, Zoe said softly, "You know what you have to do."

Emma nodded. "I have to call my dad and find out the truth."

"Okay, then," Natalia jumped to her feet and reached down to help Emma up. "We'll come with you."

Warmth filled Emma's chest. Whatever happened, she would have Natalia and Zoe. Zoe took Emma's other hand, and Emma squeezed both her cousins' hands gratefully.

Chapter Fourteen

Emma and her cousins walked along the beach to get back to Natalia and Zoe's house. With every step, Emma felt her stomach tighten and her heart sink. Soon, she would know the truth about her parents. If it was bad—if her parents were really separating—well, maybe she didn't want to know any sooner than she had to. Yet, if they weren't, she definitely wanted to know right away. And soon they would know the truth about her, because she would have to tell her dad that she had snooped at his text on her mom's phone. And that meant her mom would find out, too. Emma couldn't bear to think how disappointed her parents would be in her.

As they got closer, they could hear Aunt Alison calling them from the house, sounding impatient. Zoe and Natalia glanced at each other. "Oops," Natalia said, grimacing. "I think we're late for dinner."

Emma wiped her sweaty hands against her shorts. She felt dizzy and panicky, not at all hungry. She couldn't imagine sitting down with the big, noisy family and pretending everything was okay. "I don't think I can eat. I just want to talk to my dad. But you guys go ahead, I don't want you to get into trouble."

Natalia twined their arms together. "Don't be dumb, we're not going to leave you. You're more important than dinner."

"It's not like there won't be any food left," Zoe agreed. "Mom always makes enough for an army. We just have to sneak in without them seeing us so you can make the call."

Zoe led the way, slipping through the front door and up the stairs so quietly that no one saw or heard them from the crowded dining room. Emma's cell phone was sitting on a shelf of the bookcase closest to her air mattress. She picked it up and looked at it, her heart pounding hard. "I don't think I can do it. I'm scared."

Natalia knelt down on the air mattress to peer up into Emma's face. "You can do it, Emma. I'm sure everything is okay, but you can face the truth, whatever it is. Besides, if it's bad, there's no point in putting it off," she said.

Zoe paused and then said, "And . . . even if it is true, you're not going to lose your dad. Even if he ends up staying in Seattle, he'd never abandon you. I know that for sure."

Emma knew that it was true. Even if she had to fly back and forth across the country every summer or something, her dad would never stop loving her. Thinking of that made the ball of anxiety inside her loosen a little bit. "Okay," she said, picking up her phone. "I'm ready."

As it rang, she imagined what he might be doing—it was three thirty in Seattle, the lull between the lunch and dinner rushes at Harvest Moon. There had been plenty of afternoons when she'd come back after school at just about this time. Some of the cooks would be prepping their stations and others would be grabbing a bite to eat before they had to prepare for the first wave of dinner customers. She almost expected to feel homesick thinking of it, but it was just a good memory that felt a long, long way away.

It was the quietest and emptiest time of the day in the kitchen, a good time for the conversation she needed to have.

Her dad picked up the phone, and she could hear the low noises of the afternoon kitchen behind him. "Emma?" he said, sounding pleased. "How's it going?"

"Hi, Dad," she said. "I need to talk to you."

"Hang on," he said, sounding more serious, and she heard a door shut and the kitchen noises disappear. "Okay, shoot."

"I looked at Mom's texts," she blurted out. "She said you weren't coming here."

There was a pause. "Oh, honey. Oh, no," her dad said. "No, that isn't true at all."

Emma's breath caught in her throat. "It's not?"

"Your mom and I were fighting because we were stressed out at being so far apart. She said that out of frustration, because it was beginning to feel like it would never end. But I am coming. I never wanted you to have to worry about that. I'm sorry."

He paused, and Emma said, just checking again. "But it's not true?"

"No." His voice warmed into happiness again. "In fact, Harvest Moon has hired a chef for a trial period, and that's it—whether he works out or not, I'm done. I've booked a flight and I'm coming next week."

"Are you sure?" Emma asked. There was nothing she wanted more than for her dad to come to Waverly, but he always talked about not burning bridges. "They won't be mad if it doesn't work out and you still leave?"

"At this point, they know I've done more than they could have expected," he said. "Harvest Moon and I are on very good terms."

"Oh, good," Emma said. She hesitated, then asked, "Are you going to miss Harvest Moon?"

"Yes," her dad said. "But you know what's going to be even better? Seaview House."

"Really?" Emma said, beginning to smile.

"Absolutely," her dad said. "When I'm falling asleep in our empty apartment every night, I make up breakfast menus."

"Crepes?" Emma asked.

Her dad made a considering sound. "Definitely. And I just found a really interesting fruit soup recipe."

"Soup for breakfast?" Emma said doubtfully. "Dad, I think maybe people would rather have something more breakfast-y."

"Fruit is breakfast-y," her dad said, sounding slightly

defensive, and Emma laughed. "Anyway," he added. "One thing you can count on, an absolute promise, is that I'll be there for Seaview House Bed-and-Breakfast's grand opening."

When Emma hung up, her cousins both looked at her expectantly.

"Well?" said Natalia. "Was I right? Everything's fine?"

"Yup, Natalia, it's all about you," Zoe said, but she was smiling, and her voice didn't have the bite in it that it sometimes did when the twins argued.

"Yes—he's coming, and everything's fine," Emma said, and both her cousins cheered. "Except I have to apologize to my mom for snooping in her texts."

"Ugh." Natalia made a face. "It's hard to gather information *and* respect people's privacy. But I'm sure she'll forgive you."

"Yeah," Emma agreed. She plopped down on the air mattress, which squeaked beneath her. "I can't believe it—my dad will be here next week." She looked up at Zoe and Natalia. "Thank you," she said. "So much. I needed you to help me calm down so I could find out what was going on, and you did."

"You're welcome," Natalia said.

"That's what we're here for," said Zoe. She squeezed Emma's hand. "You're our Emma!"

Chapter Fifteen

A week later, Emma stood outside the classroom with her hands on her knees, trying to catch her breath. A hard ball of anxiety was filling her stomach and her chest, and in that moment, she wanted to be anywhere but there.

"Is Emma okay?" Caitlin asked, actually sounding worried.

"She just freaks out sometimes," Natalia said. "Can you just step back and give her some room?"

Emma hadn't been worried—until that second. They were supposed to go in front of the class in a few minutes, and it had just struck her that everyone was going to be watching.

"Listen," Zoe said, leaning in close. "*You* came up with this scene, and you put us all together—I don't think Natalia and I have *ever* done a class project together— and it's really good. Because of you."

Natalia nodded. Emma looked back and forth between them. Their eyes were warm and confident. They felt sure she could do it. She couldn't let them down.

Caitlin draped a large piece of dark fabric over Emma's shoulders like a cloak, the costume she wore in her role as the first suitor.

"Okay," Emma said. "Let's go."

Emma adjusted her beard and took a bow as the class clapped. Beside her, Natalia sank into a low, sweeping curtsy, while Caitlin dipped her head, grinning. Zoe waved at the class from one side.

Their *Catherine, Called Birdy* scene had gone very well, Emma thought. They'd remembered their lines, and the class had laughed in all the right places. Emma's two beards had stayed on when they were supposed to, and her costume changes—wrapping a length of cloth around herself in different ways—had gone smoothly. The backdrop Zoe had painted, of a fine room in a medieval gentleman's house, was colorful and elegant. Natalia had been funny, growling at Caitlin, while trying to flatter her indignant suitors into staying. And Caitlin . . .

"You were really good," Emma told Caitlin. "You seemed . . ." *Likable*, she thought. A lot more likable than she found actual Caitlin most of the time. ". . . really smart and funny," she settled on. "You seemed like Birdy was in the book."

"Well, I was saying lines from the book," said Caitlin. "Thanks, though. You were good, too."

It wasn't much, but it was the first nice thing Caitlin had ever said to her, Emma thought, and they exchanged tentative smiles. *Maybe we won't ever be best friends*, Emma thought, *but I think we can get along. And we can both be close to Natalia without getting in each other's way.* Who knew, anyway? Maybe by the time they finished high school, she and Caitlin would be like sisters.

"And I, of course, was *amazing*," Natalia said dramatically, leading the way back to their seats.

Mr. Thomas shook his head at her, looking amused, but only said, "Good job, girls," and called up the next group to present their project.

At lunch, a couple of people told them how great they'd been, but Natalia had already moved on. "You're all coming tonight, right?" she asked, looking around their lunch table. Zoe and her friends had joined them for once, pleased with the success of their projects, and the table was even more crowded than usual.

Seaview House Bed-and-Breakfast wasn't ready to be an actual bed-and-breakfast yet—most of the guest rooms weren't finished—but the public rooms were done, and Emma's mom and Aunt Alison had decided they were ready to start booking events. Tonight was just a party for family and friends, to show off how they'd fixed up Seaview House so far.

But since Waverly was a small town, Emma figured 'family and friends' meant pretty much the whole town.

After school, Emma hurried toward the kitchen, tying an apron around her waist. "Sorry I'm late, Dad," she said. "I got caught up talking to Zoe and Natalia about tonight. Mom wants us to hand around appetizers, but Natalia's sure she's going to drop them in someone's lap. Especially if she gets the hot ones."

"Well, definitely don't give her the hot ones, then," Emma's dad said, turning around from the stove. "We'll put her in charge of the fruit skewers."

Even though she was late, Emma stopped for a minute to look at her dad. He had only been back for two days, and she still got an expanding feeling of love and relief inside her chest whenever she saw him. "I'm so glad you're here," she said.

He beamed back at her. "Me, too," he said. "I don't know how I got along without my favorite sous chef for so long." Handing her a stack of paper, he added, "For instance, I need your expertise right now. Your mom left me the recipes for some finger foods she's tried out, but I'm not sure how she wanted these mushroom and feta bites. Are those folded into phyllo dough, like turnovers? Or are they open on top, like nests?"

"They're sort of pointy," Emma said. "Like the dough is a little twisted on top." She twisted her fingers, trying to show him what she meant.

"Ah, I think I've got it," her dad said, "Well, let's get chopping." He grabbed a handful of shallots from the counter. Emma pulled a box of mushrooms out of the refrigerator and cleaned them. Grabbing a knife from the knife block on the counter, she started chopping, side by side with her dad.

Practically everybody in town really must be here, Emma thought that evening, looking around at the party in full swing. Seaview House was lit with warm golden light, and flowers from the garden filled vases on the tables and on the mantel over the fireplace. Her mom and Aunt Alison's friends from high school were chattering in groups, while little kids ran in and out from the porch with Mateo and Tomás. Emma had already seen most of the kids from her class, and Natalia had abandoned her tray of fruit skewers to talk to them long ago. Caitlin, standing next to Natalia, caught Emma's eye and sent her a small, but genuine, smile.

"Coming through," Zoe said, nudging Emma in the back with a tray. "Here, you take these, and I'll go back for some more of the cheesy things. Your dad said those are going like crazy."

Emma took the tray of tiny fruit tarts. Emma liked having a purpose in the crowd. She didn't need to feel awkward with new people, she could just offer them food. "Are there forks?" she asked. "Grandma Stephenson's friends love these, but they won't eat them without forks."

"Forks," Zoe said, tucking them into Emma's apron

pocket. "I know about Grandma and her friends. No sticky fingers in the Historical Society crowd."

Emma carried her tray over to Grandma's pack of older ladies. "Doesn't that look good," one of them said, reaching for a tart. "But I think I need a fork."

"I've got it," Emma said, and rested the tray against their table to hand a fork to her as the other ladies reached for the tarts.

Grandma Stephenson and Abuelita were sitting together surrounded by their friends. As Emma steadied her tray, she overheard Grandma say, "Rosa designed a whole set of exercises to help me with my hip. I'm more limber already."

Abuelita dimpled. "I keep telling her, what she needs is to build her strength back up."

Emma's eyes met Grandma's, and Grandma gave her a tiny wink.

Grandma and Abuelita's friends had emptied her tray, and Emma wove her way through the crowd back toward the kitchen. Just as she got there, Natalia dashed up and grabbed her by the wrist.

"Hey!" Emma said, almost dropping the tray. Zoe was behind Natalia, looking resigned.

"Come on upstairs," Natalia said.

"The party's down here," Emma pointed out. "And we're supposed to stay and pass out appetizers. This crowd's starving."

"We'll come back," Natalia insisted. "And, frankly, they've gotten enough work out of us for now. We're not employees, we're their daughters."

"I'm not sure you're the right one to complain about this," Zoe said. "What did you do, carry one tray before you went off with your friends?"

"We can't just walk out," Emma said. "Everybody wants food. Besides, this is fun."

"I have an idea," Zoe said. She pulled them both into the kitchen. "More trays?" she asked Emma's dad.

"On the counter," he said. "I'm about to take a break and get out there and mingle. This should be enough to keep everybody fed for a while."

Zoe hoisted a tray in each hand—one with the mushroom things, another with some kind of creamy pinwheel that was Emma's dad's recipe—and Natalia and Emma each picked one up.

"But we have to go upstairs," Natalia said as they pushed their way back through the doors. "It's *important*."

"Voilà," Zoe said, putting her trays down on two small tables. "Problem solved: We can leave and everyone still gets fed. The ravenous hordes will find the food here."

Emma and Zoe followed Natalia to the back hall, where she nudged open the hidden door to the secret staircase. On the staircase, the noise of the crowd was muffled and, as they climbed, became only the occasional laugh in the distance.

"It looks so nice up here now!" Zoe said as they entered Emma's room.

Emma looked around with satisfaction. Her antique bed had a cozy new comforter on it, with matching curtains at the window. In the dark outside the windows, they could see the stars shining bright in the sky and the lights of a few boats traveling across the bay. Emma had hung Cousin Carolyn's sketch of the bay on the opposite wall so that she would see the water and boats whichever way she was facing.

"I miss you in our room, though," Natalia said. "I liked all of us together."

"I don't miss tripping over you every morning," Zoe said. "No offense."

"So, what's up, Natalia?" Emma asked. "What's so important that we had to leave the party?"

"Well," Natalia said, shaking back her hair dramatically. Her eyes were shining. "Tonight is a very special night. Seaview House is full of people again. Our moms have their dream business. Emma's dad is here at last. And Emma has her new room. I think we should do the cousin pact."

The cousins clasped hands, Emma in the middle, and faced the bay.

"Our days together slide like sand through our fingers," Natalia said.

Zoe chimed in. "The tides go in and the tides go out, but we stay the same."

"Not just cousins and sisters, but best friends," Emma said. "Forever." Natalia and Zoe squeezed her hands as they echoed. "Forever."

"Are you happy you moved here, Emma?" Zoe asked as she let go of Emma's hand. She looked a little wistful, as if she was thinking that it hadn't always been easy.

"Of course she is!" Natalia said indignantly.

Emma smiled. "Of course I am," she agreed. "This is where I belong."

Don't miss the next Like Sisters book!

Canine chaos comes to Seaview House!

Several dogs are staying at the family bed and breakfast with their owners. There's even going to be a wedding—with dog ring bearers! Natalia loves dogs and is eager to help out, so she offers to watch and walk all the guests' dogs. She's sure her sister, Zoe, and her cousin, Emma, will help too.

But Zoe and Emma are busy with soccer and the school play. Natalia doesn't realize she's bitten off more than she can chew until one of the dogs goes missing. If the girls can't find it, the wedding will be wrecked! Can Natalia find the runaway and save the big day?

Meet
TENNEY
Grant™

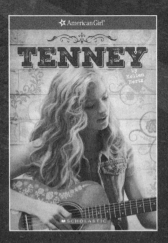

Her biggest dream is to share what's in her heart through music. Little does she know, she's about to get the opportunity of a lifetime.

★ ★ ★ ★ ★ ★ ★ ★ ★ ★ ★ ★ ★ ★ ★ ★ ★ ★

Meet
Z Yang™

Z Yang is an expert at making stop motion movies, but now she has to make a documentary. Where to start?! And will her ideas be good enough for a real film festival?